The Magic Wagon

The Magic Wagon

•

Joe R. Lansdale

Subterranean Press • 2001

JAN 1 6 2002

Subterranean Press edition
September 2001

ISBN
1-892284-81-2

Subterranean Press
P.O. Box 190106
Burton, MI 48519

email:
subpress@earthlink.net

website:
www.subterraneanpress.com

This is for Phyllis and Harlie Morton,
And Ann and Herman Kasper,
For their faith, love, and support

Chapter One

Wild Bill Hickok, some years after he was dead, came to Mud Creek for a shoot-out of sorts.

I was there. Let me tell you about it.

• • •

About an hour before sunrise, mid-July, 1909, we came rolling into Mud Creek in the Magic Wagon—Billy Bob Daniels, Old Albert, Rot Toe the Wrestling Chimpanzee, the body in the box, and me.

Night before we'd sort of snuck out of Louisiana and made the Texas border on account of some medicine Billy Bob sold this fella, telling him it would cure the piles. Which it hadn't. Not that any of us thought it would. It was just some water, coloring, and a little whisky. Well, mostly whisky.

But the fella who bought the stuff was a teetotaler and it made him drunk enough to hit his wife some and have a bellyache. And later when he passed out on the bed drunk, she sewed him up in the bedsheets, got herself a broom, and whaled the tar out of him till he was bruised enough to pass for a speckled pup.

When his wife finally did let him out from beneath the sheets he had sobered considerable, and he got to figuring on what he'd done and the fact that he had the piles bad as ever, and he came looking for Billy Bob.

Normally we'd have been long gone, as that was the smart thing in our business. Talk the crowd up good, sell them some watered whisky, smile big, wave a lot, and soon as we had their money and they were walking away, we'd pack up and hightail it out of town like a jackass with his tail on fire. Avoided a lot of unhappy customers that way.

But now and then we didn't get on our way soon enough, like this evening I'm telling you about, and usually that was because Billy Bob had spotted some gal in the crowd he'd taken a hankering to, and with the way he looked, they often took a hankering back. He was tall and lean with gray eyes and he wore his blond hair long like them old gunfighters you read about in the dime novels. Lot of times he wore guns and did trick shooting, which was something he was darned good at. But this time he didn't have no guns, and that was for the best.

He was spruced up and leaning against the wagon, ready to go gal'n, when this fella with the piles and the broom bruises shows up with a piece of cordwood in his hand and a converted .36 Navy revolver stuck in his belt. Since Billy Bob was the one who had given the talk on the medicine, told him how it could shrink them piles, it was him he wanted. He tells Billy Bob the whole sad story about how he took the medicine and it made him drunk, how he hit his wife, got sewed up in the sheets and beat, and how his piles weren't any better. In fact, he thought they might be considerable worse. Just told Billy Bob the whole shooting match. If he'd had any sense he'd have just walked up and conked Billy Bob on the head with that stove wood, but I figure he was aiming to talk him into giving him his money back before he took to raising knots.

Well, all the time this fella is telling Billy Bob his story, Billy Bob is leaning up against the Magic Wagon with a hand-rolled hanging out of his mouth unlit. When the fella finished, Billy Bob brought a match out from somewhere, lit the hand-rolled and puffed up a little cloud, squinted his eyes and said, "Ain't nothing to me."

That Billy Bob always was a considerate sort.

"It's either my money back," says the speckled pup, "or I'm going to take this here stove wood and work you up a new hat size."

"I reckon not," Billy Bob said.

That fella moved pretty quick then, swung that wood at Billy Bob's head, and Billy Bob caught his wrist with one hand and hit him in the stomach with the other, just above where that old Navy stuck out of his belt. When Billy Bob pulled his hand back, the Navy was in it and the fella was on the ground making noises like a loose treadle on a sewing machine.

Billy Bob pointed the gun and cocked back the hammer. That old cap and ball had been converted over to a cartridge loader, but it looked worn and dangerous, like it was just as likely to blow up in Billy Bob's hand as shoot that fella on the ground.

"Figure I ought to put a hole in your head," Billy Bob said.

I tensed when I heard that. Billy Bob of late had lost his sense of humor, which before had been about like a kicked badger's anyway.

But right when I thought things were going to get their ugliest, Albert said, "Mr. Billy Bob, don't reckon you ought to do that."

Albert was colored. About fifty, with snow in his short kinky hair and shoulders so wide he had to turn sideways to get inside the wagon. He looked a little bit like a bear that had been trained to wear clothes.

All the while things had been going on between Billy Bob and the fella, Albert had been standing quietly by with his arms crossed, showing about as much interest as a cow watching a couple of stumps.

"You talking to me?" Billy Bob said, glancing at Albert. Billy Bob reckoned the war wasn't over yet, and he'd never cottoned to a colored fella telling him anything. Hated it worse than anyone I'd ever seen. Once, in Kansas, I saw him beat a little colored man to his knees just because the fella brushed up against him and didn't say pardon me with enough feeling. But when he talked to Albert like that, the talk seemed mostly just talk. Somehow, Albert had the Indian sign on him, and Billy Bob, who didn't seem afraid of nothing as far as I could tell, didn't give Albert a whole lot of trouble, in spite of Albert being hired help. I sort of got the feeling there was something between them I didn't understand. Something going on I didn't have no sense about.

Even if Billy Bob wasn't scared of Albert, he wasn't shy of brains at that moment. A man Albert's size and strength — I'd once seen him set the Magic Wagon upright after it had been turned over in a storm — could take a .36 Navy slug pretty good and still get his hands on you and rip you apart like so much pine bark.

Albert's voice, which had been sharp as a knife edge, now went firm and flat. "Ain't got no right shooting this here fella on account of some stuff we sold him didn't work. It don't never work on nothing besides sober. Kill this fella and you won't have a minute's peace from the law."

"And if I decide to go ahead and do what I want?" Billy Bob asked.

"Then I'm going to have to take that pistol away from you and tie it around your neck and you'll just have to tell folks it's a bow tie."

Billy Bob looked at Albert and smiled.

Albert smiled back. They were just a couple of friendly grinners now.

I could never tell about those two. Didn't know if they were really smiling or possum smiling. But Billy Bob said, "Ah hell, I wasn't going to shoot nobody."

"No sir," Albert said, "didn't reckon you was."

Billy Bob unloaded the gun, tossed it in the street. He looked down at the fella in the dirt who was looking up. "Good drunk didn't hurt you none," Billy Bob said. "Any old battle-axe who'd put up with you deserves a hitting, and a broom whipping didn't do you no harm neither."

Billy Bob turned around and climbed in the back of the wagon, yelling, "Albert, get us out of here."

"Yes sir, Mister Billy Bob," Albert said. Billy Bob was in control again, and Albert was like a plantation slave. I couldn't figure it. I didn't say nothing. Just climbed up on the wagon beside Albert and watched him take the lines. He looked over at me and winked. "Guess Mister Billy Bob going to be leaving him another little gal hanging."

"Reckon so," I said.

"Git up there, Ishamel," Albert called to the head mule, and off we went.

I leaned over the side and looked back at the fella in the street. He was standing now, holding his stomach. He stooped to pick up his hat and gun. I turned back to watch the road.

Albert had the mules talked up pretty good now, and they were stepping on out. Which was a good thing. I figured we'd darn near seen a shooting, one way or another. And after that fella spread word around about what we'd done, it would be right wise of us to be a fair piece on down the road.

That Billy Bob seemed determined to get himself in trouble, and for some reason, Albert seemed determined to keep him out of it. Me, I was just determined and didn't know what for. From time to time I figured on leaving the Magic Wagon, going my own way. But truth was, I didn't know nothing else. And me and Albert were friends, good friends.

13

On the other hand, Billy Bob and me never had got along. We wasn't even friendly. All I knew about Billy Bob was that he'd taken me in after my parents were killed, fed me, clothed me, given me a job and some spending money. All this was on account of Albert pushed him to do it, but nonetheless, it was Billy Bob's wagon and I figured I owed him. That's all the feeling I had for Billy Bob, nothing else. Least that's the way it was until we got to Mud Creek and some new light got shed on things. Then I knew damn good and well how I felt about him.

But I'm getting ahead of myself.

• • •

So Albert drove the mules through the night, stopping only twice to let them blow, and then just for a few minutes.

Finally, just after sunup, we made Mud Creek. Good thing. The mules were tuckered out, and so were we. All that fast moving had my guts jostled something terrible, and both my legs were near asleep.

We stopped just past the sign that read MUD CREEK, and I climbed down from the wagon to stretch. Just a rawboned kid then. Seventeen, with an old gray cap and a grayer shirt and pants that had such a shine to them that they'd have blinded you had the moon or sunlight hit them just right.

Soon as my feet touched ground, I knew things were going to happen in this town. It was like a ripple had run under my feet, or maybe more like it feels when there's a real bad storm in the air and the lightning is stitching so thick it makes your hair stand up and your skin feel prickly. Mud Creek felt like a town with a soul, and a bad old soul at that.

It wasn't nothing to look at neither, there in that early morning grayness. It looked like someone had taken a handful of old ugly buildings and tossed them like dice onto a dirty hunk of ground and surrounded them with the biggest, darkest East Texas pines you'd ever seen. Most towns you come to the buildings are on either side of the main street, but here the street just sort of wandered down between the buildings as best it could. Like there wasn't no plan or nothing. Just build as you will, do as you will.

Albert climbed down, took care of the mules and came around to stand by me. He put his hands on his hips and stretched his back until it popped. When he was stretched out, he looked at the town and grimaced.

"I tell you, Little Buster, that town's full of all manner of bad spirits. It's done gone and had it a real bad life, and it ain't going to get no better."

Now I really had the shakes. Albert claimed he could feel and sometimes see spirits. He believed all things had souls, even rocks and trees. Sounded like some of the stuff I'd heard Indians say, only Albert got his beliefs from his grandfather and great-grandfather, both of which had been slaves, and the great-grandfather had been direct from Africa. He'd told Albert all manner of stories about over there. About spirits and goblins, and little short folks that lived in the woods and had poisoned arrows and such. Some of it sounded pretty wild to me, especially that stuff about the short folks, but Albert believed it all. And from the things that had happened to me since I'd teamed up with the Magic Wagon, I was beginning to believe most anything.

And I could feel the bad in Mud Creek too, though it could have been Albert's tall tales rubbing off on me. But there was the stone cold fact that I'd felt that badness before Albert even stepped down off the wagon.

I was considering on all of this, when the back door of the Magic Wagon came open and out stumbled Billy Bob, drunker than a fly in a cider barrel. He'd been right heavy into our Cure-All. He made a few steps, turned, looked down the road at the town, and said, "Well, I'll be damned." Then he passed out and hit the dirt, half a bottle of Cure-All spilling out on the ground.

Albert and me pulled him inside the wagon, laid him out on his stoop, and after Albert went out, I listened a bit to see if I could hear the wood talking like it did sometimes, but it was quiet. Which really suited me best. It gave me the rabbit hops when it talked, but I couldn't keep from listening for it just the same. I tried to tell myself wasn't nothing to it, but I knew better. Each day things seemed to get stranger and stranger with Billy Bob and the Magic Wagon, and I didn't see no letup in sight.

Since we'd fixed them busted sideboards up with them sacred trees from the Dakotas and Billy Bob had bought that rock-hard body in the box, things had gotten considerably curious. Strangest thing was this storm that had taken to following us wherever we went, though it hadn't caught up with us yet. Sometimes we got a little wind and rain from it, that sort of thing, but never the full blow. We always managed to stay about three days ahead of it. But it was like a hound dog for us, and I knew if we stayed put anywhere long enough, it would show up. And I knew too, if it wasn't for all them pines, I'd be able to look out the back of the Magic Wagon and see lightning flashing way off in the distance. When we was in Kansas, I remember being able to see it darn near all the time, and it was unsettling to always look behind you, night or day, and see lightning forks cutting across the sky, getting closer and closer, until finally you could feel the first licks of the wind and the rain.

When I first noticed the big blow was following us, I told Albert, and he knew right off what I was talking about. He'd noticed it too, and like me, he figured it was either them sacred trees or that body in the box that was responsible, since both was supposed to have a curse on them.

Course, Billy Bob wouldn't have such talk. He just laughed. "Ain't nothing following us but your own silly daydreams," he'd say. But I'd seen him watching the skies from time to time, and he never let us stay in any place more than a night, and we always moved out real early the next morning, and he made us move faster than you'd really have a need to unless something was behind us.

In fact, I sort of think he was glad that wife-beat fella with the stove wood and the pistol came along, as that gave him a good excuse to put a few more hours between him and that storm, and he could tell himself it didn't have nothing to do with fear of curses and such.

But he didn't fool me. He was as worried and scared of that storm as me and Albert, and he'd taken to drinking a whole lot since the Dakotas and sometimes he cried out in his sleep and shook like a wet pup.

"Them ole Injun spirits in the wood, they talking to him," Albert would tell me. And Albert believed that. He'd quit sleeping inside the wagon since we'd put in those sideboards from the sacred trees, and you couldn't hardly get him inside of it unless it was to do business of some sort, or it was raining real hard.

Me, I'd lay there on my stoop at night—Billy Bob across the way—and listen to that wood moan and groan, and sometimes, when the back door was open—which was most of the time in the summer—and the moonlight was thick, I'd think I could see eyes looking out of that wood at me, or mouths moving. But when I'd light a match for a look-see, it would just be pine knots. One night I even thought something had reached out of the wood to take hold of my hand, but when I jerked awake, I didn't find nothing there.

And there was the body in the box. Thinking on that thing didn't improve my sleep neither. The mere thought of it gave me a cold rigor.

Considering all this as I stood there in the wagon, I turned to look at it and got a start. The box was propped up where it always was, but the lid was open and the body was gone.

My back felt like a batch of big spiders were crawling up it. I turned and looked around the dark wagon, saw the shape at Billy Bob's feet, between the foot of his stoop and the wall by the door. It had been there all along. Albert and I just hadn't noticed it. That crazy drunk had pulled it out of the box and propped it up so it could look over him, like some kind of bodyguard.

My eyes were used to the dark enough now that I could see it, but fortunate for me I couldn't see so good I could make out its features—the ones it had left. Even when Billy Bob showed it to folks and said his talk about it, I never really looked straight at it. I somehow figured if I did it would get the whammy in on me, or something. No matter from where you looked at it, it always seemed to be looking at you with them hollow sockets and that half-open mouth with the little thin teeth gone copper-colored and yellow. And I think the wisps of hair that stuck out in spots on the skull like the last down on a near plucked goose were worse. And I didn't care for them pistols that were clenched in them skeleton fists. They looked too shiny and too well-oiled and ready to go. Course, it was Billy Bob that put hinges in the corpse's elbows so he could set the guns where he wanted them, but the thought of that thing standing there with them old pistols clutched in its bones made me want to wet myself.

I believed that story the Indian had told Billy Bob about whose body that was, and about the curse that was on it. There was some that would argue Wild Bill Hickok was in the cemetery at Deadwood, but I wouldn't be one of them. They ever dig his grave up they're going to find there ain't nothing in there but worms and dirt. Wild Bill rides with us.

I went out of there, staying as far to the other side of the door as I could, and stepped out into the morning light. When I was breathing better, I went around to the side of the wagon and peeled up the tarp and looked in on Rot Toe.

The old ape looked at me and let out a hoot, but didn't move. Big as he was, he looked tired and miserable. He'd been that way a lot lately. Albert says it's because he's getting old and Billy Bob don't treat him right, poking him with sticks and such like he does. He thinks Billy Bob ought to let Rot Toe cut the wrestling act, just start being there for folks to look at for a nickel a peek. Albert would like to keep him on a long chain when we were in a town, and rest of the time let him run loose on the wagon, ride up front with us. Billy Bob don't see it that way, though. He's scared of Rot Toe.

And good reason. He's picked at that ape enough, that he can't be alone with him. Rot Toe, given half the chance, would tear Billy Bob apart.

Well, Albert's ideas seemed good to me, Rot Toe being old and all, though when he got that muzzle and them gloves put on him, and got out there to wrestle two-hundred-and-forty-pound men, he didn't look old then, gray hairs or not. He just looked big and strong and scary, and the way he slung them fellas around, it was hard to believe he didn't weigh but a little over a hundred pounds.

"You okay, old man?" I said.

Rot Toe let out that little hoot again, brought his hand up and touched his face. If he'd been willing to move and come across the cage, he'd probably have reached out and touched me. Touching himself or someone else, unless it was Billy Bob, always seemed to make him feel better. And reckon if he could touch Billy Bob in the way he wanted, he'd have felt mighty good then too.

"Take it easy, old fella," I said, and I lowered the tarp.

I looked off to the east, and now that I was out of the wagon, I could see the sky above the pines. I looked for lightning to be sewing through the sky like some kind of crazy seamstress, but there wasn't nothing there. Didn't hear no thunder neither, but I knew that storm hadn't given up on us yet. We'd see sign of it soon.

I went around to the front of the wagon, up to the head mule, Ishamel. Albert was there, rubbing the old critter on the forehead and looking out at the silly-laid-out town.

"Well, Little Buster," he said, "what'cha think?"

"I don't like it none."

"Me neither, but Mister Billy Bob is set."

"To hell with Billy Bob," I said braver than I felt. "I got a feeling that whatever bad that's been waiting to happen to this town has been waiting on us."

"That may be," Albert said with that accepting way of his, "but Mister Billy Bob's the one buys the bacon."

I didn't say anything back. Albert went around and climbed on the wagon and picked up the lines. I got up on my side and Albert softly called to the mules and we started rolling into Mud Creek proper, and the closer we got the lighter it got, and the more it looked like any other little town, except for the way it was laid out, and I could see people moving around now, starting their day, and it looked just as normal as could be.

But that didn't make me feel no better.

Chapter Two

It was a hot day already and I thought about that and wished I'd left Rot Toe's tarp up. Sweat was coming from beneath the brim of my cap and streaming down my face, running into the edge of my mouth. It tasted like salt, dirt, and sadness, mostly sadness, because sweat always reminds me of tears.

There was the smell of animal lots on the warm wind, and it wasn't too bad. Not bad like some of the cow towns we'd been in. So bad in some that the stink made you have to lean over and throw up what you'd eaten. This was small-town animal stink, not the months old, ankle-deep mess of a Kansas cow lot. In fact, it was almost pleasant. Reminded me that I was once again in my old stomping grounds, East Texas, and that the place where I'd grown up wasn't all that far away.

And though I didn't want to think on it, that barnyard smell took me back a few years, back to the baddest old winter we'd ever seen, the winter I came to believe in signs and omens. The winter I turned fifteen.

• • •

It had come a rare snow that year, and even rarer for East Texas. It had actually stuck to the ground and got thick. Along came the wind, colder than ever, and it turned the snow to ice. It was beautiful, like sugar-and-egg white icing on a cake, but it wasn't nothing to enjoy after the excitement of first seeing it come down. I had to get out in it and do chores, and that made me wish for a lot of sunshine and a time to go fishing.

Third day after it snowed and things had gotten real icy, I was out cutting firewood from the woodlot and I found a madman in a ditch.

I'd already chopped down a tree and was trimming the limbs off of it, waiting for Pap, who was coming across the way with a crosscut so we could saw it up into firewood sizes. While I was trimming, I heard a voice.

"Got a message. Get out of this ditch, I got a message."

Clutching the axe tight, I went over and looked in the ditch, and there was a man lying there. His face was as blue as Mama's eyes, and Papa says they're so blue the sky looks white beside them, even on its best day. His long, oily hair had stuck to the ground and frozen there so that the clumped strands looked like snakes or fat worms trying to find holes to crawl into. There were icicles hanging off his eyelids and he was barefoot.

I screamed for Pap. He tossed down the saw and came running fast as he could on that ice. We got down in the ditch, hauled the fella up, pulling out some of his frozen hair in the doing. He was wearing a baggy old pair of faded black suit pants with the rear busted out, and his butt was hanging free and drawerless. It was darker than his face, looked a bit like a split, overripe watermelon gone dark in the sun. His feet and hands were somewhere between the blue of his face and the blue-black of his butt. The shirt he had on was three sizes too big, and when Papa and I had him standing, the wind came a-whistling along and flapped the fella's shirt around him till he looked like a scarecrow we were trying to poke in the ground.

We got him up to the house, and stretched him out on the kitchen table. He looked like he'd had it. He didn't move an inch. Just laid there, eyes closed, breathing slow.

Then, all of a sudden, his eyes snapped open and he shot out a bony hand and grabbed Papa by the coat collar. He pulled himself to a sitting position until his face was even with Papa's and said, "I got a message from the Lord. You are doomed, brother, doomed to the wind, cause it's gonna blow you away." Then he closed his eyes, laid back down and let go of Papa's shirt.

"Easy," Papa said. But about that time the fella gave a shake, like he was having a rigor, then he went still as a turnip. Papa felt for a pulse and put his ear to the scarecrow's chest, looking for a heartbeat. From the expression on Papa's face, I could tell he hadn't found any.

"He's dead, Papa?"

"Couldn't get no deader, son," Papa said, lifting his head from the man's chest.

Mama, who'd been standing off to the side watching, came over. "You know him, Harold?" she asked.

"Think this is Hazel Onin's son," Papa said.

"The crazy boy?" she said.

"I just seen him once, but I think it's him. They had him on a leash out in the yard one summer, had this colored fella leading him around, and the boy was running on all fours, howling and trying to lift his leg to pee on things. His pants was all wet."

"How pitiful," Mama said.

I knew of Hazel Onin's boy, but if he had a name I'd never heard it. He'd always been crazy, but not so crazy at first they couldn't let him run free. He was just considered mighty peculiar. When he was eighteen he got religion worse than smallpox and took to preaching.

Right after he turned twenty, he tried to rape a little high yeller gal he was teaching some Bible verses to, and that's when the Onins throwed him in that attic room, locked and barred the windows. If he'd been out of that room since that time, I'd never heard of it, other than what Papa had said about the leash and wetting himself and all.

I'm ashamed of it now, but when I was twelve or thirteen, me and some other boys used to have to walk by there on our way to and from school, and the madman would holler out from his barred windows at us. "Repent, cause you all gonna have a bad fall," then he'd go to singing some old gospel songs and it gave me the jitters cause there was an echo up there in that attic, and it made it seem that there was someone else singing along with him. Someone with a voice as deep and trembly as Old Man Death might have.

Freddy Clarence used to pull down his pants, bend over and show his naked butt to the madman's window, and we'd follow his lead on account of not wanting to be called a chicken. Then we'd all take off out of there running, hooping and hollering, pulling our pants and suspenders up as we ran.

But we'd quit going by there a long time back, as had almost everyone else in town. They moved Main Street when the railroad came through on the other side, and from then on the town built up over there. They even tore down and rebuilt the schoolhouse on that side, and there wasn't no need for us to come that way no more. We could cut shorter by going another way. And after that, I mostly forgot about the madman prophet.

"It's such a shame," Mama said. "Poor boy."

"It's a blessing, is what it is," Papa said. "He don't look like he's been eating so good to me, and I bet that's because the Onins ain't feeding him like they ought to. They figure him a shame and a curse from God, and they've treated him like it was his fault his head ain't no good ever since he was born."

"He was dangerous, Harold," Mama said. "Remember that little high yeller girl?"

"Ain't saying he ought to have been invited to no church social. But they didn't have to treat him like an animal."

"Guess it's not ours to judge," Mama said.

"Damn sure don't matter now," Papa said.

"What do you think he meant about that thing he said, Papa?" I asked. "About the wind and all?"

"Didn't mean a thing, son. Boy didn't have a nut in his shell is all. Crazy talk. Go on out and hitch up the wagon and I'll get him wound up in a sheet. We'll take him back to the Onins. Maybe they'll want to stuff him and put him in the attic window so folks can see him as they walk or ride by. Maybe they could charge two bits to come inside and gawk at him. Pull his arm with a string so it looks like he's waving at them."

"That's quite enough, Harold," Mama said. "Don't talk like that in front of the boy."

Papa grumbled something, went out of the room for a sheet, and I went out to the barn and hitched the mules up. I drove the wagon up to the front door, went in to help Papa carry the body out. Not that it really took both of us. He was as light as a big, empty corn husk. But somehow, the two of us carrying him seemed a lot more respectable than just tossing him over a shoulder and slamming him down in the wagon bed.

We took the body over to the Onins, and if they were broke up about it, I missed the signs. They looked like they'd just finally gotten some stomach tonic to work, and had made that long put off and much desired trip to the outhouse.

Papa didn't say nothing stern to them, though I expected him to, since he wasn't short on honest words. But I figure he didn't see any need in it at that point. The fella was dead.

Mrs. Onin stood in the doorway all this time, didn't come out to the wagon bed while the body was there. After Mr.

Onin unwound the sheet and took a look at the madman's face, said what a sad day it was and all, he asked us if we'd mind putting the body in the toolshed.

We did, and when we got back to the wagon, Mrs. Onin was waiting by it. Mr. Onin offered us a dollar for bringing the body home, but of course, Papa didn't take it.

Before we climbed up on the wagon, Mrs. Onin said, "He'd been yelling from upstairs all morning, saying how an angel from God wearing a suit coat and a top hat had brought him a message he was supposed to pass on. Kept saying the angel was giving him a test to see if he deserved heaven after what he'd done to that little girl."

Papa climbed on the wagon, took hold of the lines. With his head, he motioned me up.

"Then we didn't hear nothing no more," Mr. Onin said. "I went up there to check on him and he'd pulled the bars out of one of the windows and got out. I don't reckon how he did that, as he'd never been able to do it before, and them bars was as sturdy as the day I put them in, no rotten wood around the sills or nothing."

Papa had taken out his pocket knife and tobacco bar, and he was cutting a chaw off of it. "Reckon you went right then to the sheriff to tell him your boy run off," Papa said, and there was an edge to his voice, like when he finds me peeing out back too close to the house.

"Naw," Mr. Onin said, looking at the ground, "I didn't. Figured cold as it was, he'd come back."

"Don't matter none now, does it?" Papa said.

"No," Mr. Onin said. "He's out of his misery now."

"Them's as true words as you've spoke," Papa said.

"I'll be getting that sheet back to you," Mr. Onin said.

"Don't want it," Papa said. He clucked up the mules and we started off.

When we were out of earshot of the house, I said, "Papa, you reckon they thought that crazy fella would go back because he was cold?"

"Why in hell would he want to go back to that attic? Even if it might have been warm."

We didn't say anything else until we got home, then wasn't none of the talking about the madman or the Onins. Mama didn't even mention it after she saw Papa's face.

Just before supper, Papa went out on the porch to smoke his pipe, and I went out to the barn to toss some hay to the mules and the milk cow. I was tossing it, smelling that animal smell, thinking about how it reminded me of my whole life, that smell. Reminded me of Mama and Papa, warm nights with very little breeze, cold nights with the fire stoked up big and warm, late suppers, tall tales in front of the fireplace, standing on the porch or looking out of the windows at the morning, noon or night, spring, summer, fall, or winter. And that smell, always there, like a friend who had some peculiar, if not bad-smelling, toilet water. It was in the floorboards of the house, on the yard, thick in the barn. A smell that even now moves me backwards and forwards in time, confuses me on which are the truths and which are the lies of my memory.

So there I was, throwing hay, thinking this fine life would go on forever, and all of a sudden, I felt it before it happened.

I quit tossing hay, turned to look out the barn door. It was like I was looking at a painting, things had gone so still. The sky had turned yellow. The late birds quit singing and the mules and the milk cow turned their heads to look outdoors too.

Way off I heard it, a sound like a locomotive making the grade, burning that timber. Only there wasn't a track within ten miles of us. Outside the sky went from yellow to black, from still to windy. Pine straw, dust and all manner of things began whipping by. I knew exactly what was happening.

Twister.

I dropped the pitchfork, dove for the inside of an old shovel-scoop mule sled, and no sooner had I hit face down and put my hands over my head, then it slammed into the barn.

I caught a glimpse of a cow flying by, legs splayed like she thought she could stop the tug of the wind easy as she could stop the tug of a rope. Then the cow was gone and the sled started to move.

After that, everything happened so quickly I'm not certain what I saw. Lots of things flying by, for sure, and I could hardly breathe. The sled might have gone as high as thirty feet, cause when I came down it was hard. Hadn't been for the ice, I'd probably have been driven into the ground like a cork in a bottle. But the sled hit the ice at an angle and started sliding, throwing up dirty, hard snow on either side of me. Pieces of ice hit me in the face and the sled fetched up against something solid, a stump probably, and I went flying out of it, hit the ice, whirled around like a fly in a greasy skillet, came to rest in the ditch where I found the madman.

I passed out for a while, and I dreamed. Dreamed I was in the sled again, flying through the air, and there was our house, lifting up from the ground, floor and all. It flew right past me, rising fast. When it moved in front of me, I glimpsed Mama. She was standing at the window. All the glass was blown out, and she was clinging to the sill with both hands. Her eyes were as big and blue as her china saucers, and her red hair had come undone and was blowing and whipping around her head like a brush fire.

The house shot on up, and when I looked up to see, there wasn't nothing but whirling blackness with little chunks of wood and junk disappearing into it.

"Mama," I said, and I must have said it a lot of times, cause that's what brought me to. The sound of my own voice calling Mama.

I tried to stand, but my ankle wasn't having it. It hurt like hell, and when I looked down, I saw my boot and sock had been ripped off by the blow, and the ankle was as big as a coiled cottonmouth snake.

I put a hand on the edge of the ditch, dug my fingers through the ice, and pulled myself up, taking some of the skin off my naked foot as I did. It was so cold the flesh had frozen to the ground and it had peeled off like sweet-gum bark.

Once I was out of the ditch, I started crawling across the ice, dragging my useless foot behind me. Little chunks of skin came off my palms, so I had to pull myself forward on my coat-sleeved forearms.

I hadn't gone far before I found Papa. He was sitting in his rocking chair, and in one hand he held his pipe and it was still smoking. The porch the chair had been sitting on was gone, but Papa was rocking gently in what was left of the wind. And the pitchfork I'd tossed aside before diving into the sled was sticking out of his chest like it had growed there. I didn't see a drop of blood. His eyes were open and staring, and every time that chair rocked forward, he seemed to look and nod at me.

Behind Papa, where the house ought to have been, wasn't nothing. It was like it hadn't never been built. I quit crawling and started crying. Did that till there wasn't nothing in me to cry, and the cold started making me so numb I just wanted to lay there and freeze at Papa's feet like an old dog. I felt like if I wasn't his killer, I was at least a helper in the murder, having tossed down the very pitchfork the twister had thrown at him.

It started to rain little ice pellets, and somehow the pain of those things pounding on me gave me the will to crawl toward a heap of hay that had been chunked there by the wind. By the time I got to the pile and looked back, Papa wasn't rocking no more. Those runners had froze to the ground and his black hair had turned white from the ice that had stuck to it.

I worked my way into the hay and tried to pull as much of it over me as I could. Doing that wore me completely out, and I fell asleep wondering about what had happened to Mama, hoping she was still alive.

The wind picked up again, took most of the hay away, but by then I didn't give a damn. I awoke remembering that I'd had that dream about Mama and the house again. Even though I didn't have much hay on me, it didn't seem so cold anymore. I figured it was either warming up, or I was getting used to it. Course, wasn't neither of them things. I was freezing to death, and would have too, if not for Mr. Parks and his boys.

Mr. Parks was our nearest neighbor, about three miles east. Turned out he had been chopping wood when the sky went yellow. Later he told me about it, and he said it was as strange as a blue-eyed hound dog, and unlike any twister he'd ever seen. Said the yellow sky went black, then this dark cloud grew a tail and came a-waggin' out of the heavens like a happy dog, getting thicker as it dipped. When it touched down, he figured the place it hit was right close to our farm, so he hitched up a wagon and came on out.

It was slow going for him and his two boys, on account of the ice and them having to stop now and then to clear the road of blown-over trees and a dead deer once. But they made it to our place about dark, and Mr. Parks said the first thing he saw was Papa in that rocker. He said it was like the stem of Papa's pipe was pointing to where I lay, partly in, partly out of that hay.

They figured me for croaked at first, I looked so bad. But when they saw I hadn't gone under, they loaded me in the wagon, covered me in some old feed sacks and a couple of half-wet blankets, and started out of there.

That foot of mine was broke bad. The doctor came out to the Parks' place, set it, and didn't charge me a cent. He said that was on account of he owed Papa for a bushel of taters from last fall, but I knew that was just one of them friendly white lies. Doc Ryan hadn't never owed nobody nothing.

Mr. and Mrs. Parks offered me a place to stay after the funeral, but I told them I'd go back to our place and try and make a go of it there.

Johnny Parks, who used to whip the hell out of me twice a week on them weeks we both managed to go a full week to school, made me a pair of solid crutches out of hickory, and I went to Papa's funeral on them.

Mama, as if there was something to my dream, wasn't never found, and for that matter, they couldn't hardly find no pieces of the house. There was plenty of barn siding around, but of the house there was only a few floorboards, some wood shingles, and some broken glass. Maybe it's silly, but I like to think that old storm just come and got her and hauled her off to a better place, like that little gal in that book *The Wizard of Oz*.

Mr. Parks made Papa a tombstone out of a piece of river slate, chiseled some nice words on it:

HERE LIES HAROLD FOGG, KILT BY A TORNADER? AND HERE LIES THE MEMRY OF GLENDA FOGG WHO WAS CARRIED OFF BY THAT SAME TORNADER AND WASN'T NEVER FOUND, NOT EVEN THE PIECES.

Beneath that were some dates on when they was born and died, and a line about them being survived by one son, Buster Fogg, meaning me, of course.

Over the protests of Mr. and Mrs. Parks, I had them take me out to our place and I set up a tent there. They left me a lot of food and some hand-me-down clothes from their boys, then they went off saying they'd be back to check on me right regular. Mrs. Parks cried some and Mr. Parks offered me some money and the loan of his mule, but I said I had to think on it.

This tent Mr. Parks gave me was a good one, and I managed to get around well enough on my crutches to gather barn siding and what tools and nails I could find, and I built a floor in it. I could have got Mr. Parks and his boys to do that for me, but I couldn't bring myself to it, not after all they'd done. And besides, I had my pride. Matter of fact, now that I think on it, that was about all I had. That and the place.

Well, it took me a couple of days to do what should have taken a few hours on account of having to pull nails out of boards and reuse them, but I got the tent fixed up real good and cozy finally. It wasn't no replacement for the house and Mama and Papa, but it was better than stepping on a tack or getting jabbed in the eye with a pointed stick.

I wished I could have turned back time some, been in our house. I'd even have liked to have heard Mama fussing over how much firewood Papa should have laid in, which was one of the few things he was always a little lazy on, and was finally glad to pass most of the job along to me. I could hear Mama telling him as she looked at the last few sticks of stove wood, "I told you so."

On the morning after I'd spent my first night on my finished floor, I got up to take a good look at things, and see what I could manage on crutches.

There were dead chickens lying about, like feather dusters, pieces of wood and one mule lying on his back, legs sticking up in the air like a table blowed over. Didn't see a sign of the other mule or the cows.

Wasn't none of this something I hadn't already seen, but now with the flooring in, and my immediate comfort taken care of, I found I just couldn't face picking up dead chickens and burning a mule carcass.

I went back inside the tent and felt sorry for myself, as that's all there was to do, besides eat, and I'd done that till I was about to pop. I wasn't such a great reader, but right then I wished I had me a book of some kind, but what books we'd had had been blowed away with the house.

About a week went by, and I'd maybe got half the chickens picked up and tossed off in the ditch by the woodlot, and gotten the mule burned to nothing besides bones, when this slick-looking fella in a buckboard showed up.

"Howdy there young feller," he said, climbing down from his rig. "You must be Buster Fogg."

I admitted I was, and up close I seen that snazzy black suit and narrow brim hat he had on were even snappier than they'd looked at a distance. The hat and suit were dark as fresh charcoal, and the pants had creases in them sharp enough to cut your throat. And he was all smiles. He looked to have more teeth than Main Street had bricks.

"Glad to catch you home," he said, and he took off his hat and held it over his chest as if in silent prayer.

"Whatsit I can do for you?" I asked. "Maybe you'd like to come in the tent, get out of this cold?"

"No, no. What I have to say won't take but a moment. My name is Purdue. Jack Purdue. I'm the banker from town."

Well, right off I knew what it was and I didn't want to hear it, but I knew I was going to anyhow.

"Your father's bill has come due, son, and I hate it something awful, and I know it's a bad time and all, but I'm going to need that money by about" — he stopped for a moment to look generous — "say noon tomorrow. Least half."

"I ain't got a penny, Mr. Purdue," I said. "Papa had the money, but everything got blowed away in the storm. If you could just give me some time—"

He put his hat on and looked real sad about things, almost like it was his farm he was losing.

"I'm afraid not, son. It's an awful duty I got, but it's my duty."

I told him again about the money blowing away, how Papa had saved it up from selling stuff during the farm season, doing odd jobs and all, and that I could do the same, providing he gave my leg time to heal and me to get the work. Just to play on his sympathy some, I then went on to tell him the whole horrible truth about how Papa was killed and Mama blowed away like so much outhouse paper, and when I got through I figured I'd told it real good, cause his eyes looked a little moist.

"That," he said, not hardly able to speak, "is without a doubt the saddest story I've ever heard. And of course I knew about it, son, but somehow, hearing it from you, the last survivor of the Fogg family, makes it all the more dreadful."

He kind of choked up there on the end of his words, and I figured I had hold of him pretty good, so I throwed in how us Foggs had pride and all, and that I'd never let an owed bill go unpaid, and if he'd just give me the time to raise the money, he'd have it in his hand before long.

He told me he was tore all to hell about it, but business was business, sad story or not. And as he wiped some tears out of his eyes with the back of his hand, he told me he would give me until tomorrow evening instead of noon, because he reckoned someone who'd been through what I had deserved a little more time.

"But that ain't enough," I said.

"Sorry, son, that's the best I can do, and that goes against the judgment of the bank. I'm sticking my neck out to do that."

"You are the bank, Purdue," I said. "Who you fooling? It ain't me. We all know you're the bank."

"I understand your grief, your great torment," he said, just like one of the characters from some of them dime novels Papa bought from time to time, "but business is business."

"You said that."

"Yes I did, young sir." With that, Purdue turned and walked back to his buckboard. He called out to me as I stood there leaning defeated on my crutches. "I tell you, son, that is the saddest story I've ever heard, and I've heard some. Tragic. This will hang over my head like the shining sword of Damocles from here on out, right over my head," he showed me exactly where it would be hanging with his hand, "until my dying day."

He stood there with one foot on the buckboard step a moment, looking as downcast as a young rooster without any hens, then he climbed up and cracked the whip gently over the heads of the horses. There must have been some pretty heavy tears in his eyes as he left, cause when he turned the buckboard around, the left wheels rolled right across Papa's grave.

My farming days were over before they even got started. And I'll tell you, right then and there, I decided I wasn't going to pick up another dead chicken to make the place look nicer. In fact, I went over to the ditch, got the ones I'd throwed down there out and chunked them around sorta like they'd been. Then I went back to my tent and wished I hadn't burned that old dead mule up. It was all mighty depressing.

The smartest thing to have done was go on over to Mr. Parks's place, even if it did take me all damned day on crutches, but I just couldn't. Us Foggs had our pride and I didn't want no handout. No one taking care of me when I was old enough to take care of my ownself. I decided to set out for town, get me a job there, make my own way. Even if I couldn't save the farm, I could start me some kind of living. There was probably something I could work at until my leg healed up and I got me a solid job.

I figured if I started early, like tomorrow morning, I could make town by nightfall, crutches or not. I'd most likely fall down and bust it a few times, but that didn't matter none.

Well, as I said, us Foggs are proud, and maybe just a bit ' stupid, so come morning I put some hard bread, jerked meat, and dried fruit in a sack, and saying adios to the dead chickens, the mule bones, and Papa's grave, I started crutching on out of there.

I must have fallen down a half-dozen times before I got to the road, but when I was on it I could crutch along better because there was a lot less ice there.

By noon my underarms were so sore from the rubbing of the crutches, they were bleeding and making blisters that kept popping as I went. Instead of making it to town by nightfall, I was beginning to think I'd be lucky to make it by next year's Thanksgiving. In fact, I was counting on dying at that moment, just keeling over beside the road there and kicking out the last of my worries.

I stopped, sat down on a rock and my coattails, ate some bread and jerky, and fretted things over. Thinking back on it now, I'm surprised I didn't hear it coming before I did. Guess I was wrapped up in my lunch and my thinking. But I finally caught sound of this tinkling, and when I looked up I seen it was bells and harness I had heard, and the harness was attached to eight big mules pulling a bright, red wagon driven by a big colored man wearing a long, dark coat and a top hat. When the sun hit his teeth they flashed like a pearl-handled revolver.

As the wagon made a little curve in the road, I got a glimpse at the side, and I could see there was a cage fixed there, balancing out the barrels of water and supplies on the other side.

At first, I thought what was in the cage was a deformed colored fella, but when it got closer, I seen it was some kind of animal covered in black fur. It was about the scariest, ugliest damned thing I'd ever seen.

Right then I was feeling a mite less proud than I had been earlier that morning, so I got them crutches under my sore arms and hobbled out into the road waving a hand at the wagon. I was aiming on getting a ride or getting run slap over so I could end the torture. I didn't feel like I could crutch another mile.

The wagon slowed and pulled alongside me. The driver yelled, "Whoa, you old ugly mules," and the harness bells ceased to shake.

I could see the animal in the cage good now, but I still couldn't figure on what it was. There was some yellow words painted above the cage that said, "THE MAGIC WAGON," and to the right of the cage was a little sign with some fancy writing on it that read: "Magic Tricks, Trick Shooting, Fortune Telling, Wrestling Ape, Side Amusements, Medicine For What Ails You, And All At Reasonable Prices."

Sounded pretty good to me.

"You look like you could use a ride, white boy," the big man said.

"Yes sir, I could at that," I said.

"You don't yes-sir a nigger." I turned to see who had said that, and there was this fella standing in faded, red long johns and moccasins with blond hair down to his shoulders and a skimpy little blond mustache over his lip. He had his arms crossed, holding his elbows against the cold. He'd obviously come out of the back of the wagon, but he'd walked so quiet I hadn't even known he was there till he spoke.

When I didn't say nothing, he added, "This here's my wagon. He's just a nigger that works for me. I say who rides and who don't, and I say you don't."

"I got some jerky, canned taters, and beans I can trade for a ride, and I'll sit up there on the seat."

"If you was riding you sure would," the blond man said. "But you ain't riding." He turned back to the wagon and I noticed the flap of his long johns were down. I snickered a little, and he turned to stare at me. He had eyes like a couple of big nail heads, cold, flat, and gray. "I don't need no beans and taters," he said sharply, and turned back to the wagon.

"He can ride up here with me if he's got a mind to," the colored man said.

The white fella spun around and came stomping back. "What did you say?"

"I said he could ride up here with me if he's got a mind to," the colored man said, moving his lips real slow like, as if he was talking to an idiot. "It's too cold for a boy to be out here, especially one on crutches."

"You don't say," said the blond man. "You're getting awfully uppity for a nigger who works for me."

"Maybe I is," the colored fella said. "And it worries me something awful, Mister Billy Bob. I get so worried abouts it I can't get me no good sleep at night. When I lays myself down I just keep tossing and turning, wondering if Mr. Billy Bob is put out with me, and if I truly is getting uppity."

Mister Billy Bob pointed his finger at the colored fella and shook it. "Keep it up, nigger. Just keep it up and you're going to wake up with a crowd of buzzards on you. Hear?"

"I hear," said the colored man, and it was almost a yawn.

Billy Bob started back for the wagon again, gave me a glimpse of his exposed butt, turned, and came back. He shook his finger at the colored fella again. "Albert," he said, "you and me, we're going to have to have a serious Come-to-Jesus

Meeting, get some things straight about who's the nigger and who ain't."

"I do need me some pointers on that, Mister Billy Bob. I get a trifle confused sometimes and it just sets me to shuffling my feet trying to figure on the straight of it."

Billy Bob stood there for a moment, like he was going to stare Albert down off the wagon seat, but finally he gave up. "All right," he said to me. "You can ride, but it's going to cost you them beans and taters, hear?"

I nodded.

This time Billy Bob turned and went inside the wagon, the moon of his butt my last sight of him for a while, the slamming of the wagon door my last sound.

I turned and looked up at Albert. He was leaning down with a big hand extended. Just before I took it, I got me another look at the critter in the cage, and when he looked at me, he peeled back his lips to show his teeth, like maybe he was smiling.

When I was on the seat beside Albert, he said, "That Mister Billy Bob's gonna need to get them buttons fixed on the seat of his drawers, ain't he?"

We laughed at that.

After we got moving good, Albert said, "You keep them beans and taters, boy. Taters upsets my stomach, and beans, they make Mister Billy Bob fart something awful. Just ain't no being around him."

"That's good about them beans and taters," I said, "cause I ain't got none. All I got in this bag is some hard bread and jerked meat."

Albert let out a roar, like that was the funniest thing he'd ever heard. I could tell right then and there he didn't have no real respect for Billy Bob.

"That critter in the cage?" I asked. "Is that some kind of bear what caught on fire or something?"

Albert laughed again. "Naw, it ain't no bear. That there is a jungle ape. Comes from the same place as all us colored. Africa. They calls him a chimpanzee. Name's Rot Toe on account of he got him some kind of disease once and one of his toes on his right foot rotted off. Least that's what the fella who sold him to Billy Bob said."

I remembered the sign I'd read on the side of the wagon. "Wrestling ape," I said. "That thing wrestles?"

"Now you got it," Albert said.

I found a place for my crutches and the food bag, then I leaned back with my hands in my lap.

"You look a might bushed, little peckerwood. You wants to lay your head against my shoulder to rest, you go right ahead."

"No thanks," I said. But we hadn't gone too far down the road when I just couldn't keep my eyes open no more and I realized just how tired I really was. I lolled my head on Albert's big shoulder. I could smell the clean wool of his coat. And wasn't no time at all until I was asleep.

Chapter Three

I was thinking on this, feeling sorry for myself, when Albert brought me out of it.

"Best get your butt down from here and get to doing."

I'd been so lost in my thoughts, I hadn't noticed we'd stopped. We were under a big oak that grew out to the edge of the street, and around the oak were curled vines big as well ropes. Out to the right of the tree was a big clearing. It looked to have been made by fire. It was just the place for us to have our show.

Behind the clearing, and to the left of the oak, there was nothing but woods. And I do mean woods. It was thick with all manner of brush and brambles. It was just another thing that got me to thinking on the town and how odd it looked. Even the woods around it seemed different from any I'd seen before, and I found myself not wanting to stare out there for long for fear of seeing something I didn't want to see.

I got down and went around to Rot Toe's cage, limping as I went. That foot that had been broken got stiff when I rode too long or, on the other hand, walked on it too much.

I pulled back the tarp and let some fresh air in on the ape, and he grunted at me. There in the sharp, morning light, as the twilight died and the day came in, he suddenly, and for the first time, looked more than tired and old to me, he looked pathetic.

I said some words to him, got his leash off the top of the cage and used my key to let him out. He took my hand and walked with me around to the other side, and I put his leash on him without any trouble. While I did, he stood staring out at those woods, making soft sounds. He didn't care for them any better than I did.

Albert had come around and I said how I didn't like the woods and neither did Rot Toe.

"There ain't a thing to like about them," he said, and he didn't look out there when he said it. "You stay out of 'em, Little Buster, you hear?"

"Yes sir," I said.

Albert smiled at me. "You know what Billy Bob says?"

"Yeah." And we said it together, "You don't yes-sir a nigger."

"All right, boy," Albert said. "Get up there on the wagon and get them posters, start putting them up. And you're going to need to talk to the sheriff."

"Me? That's Billy Bob's job."

"He ain't rightly in the condition to do it. And you might as well get used to it, cause he's going to make it your job anyhow."

"How do you know he is?"

"I know Billy Bob, and the less work he has to do the happier man he is. He always finds me a new job or two at the end of the month, don't he?"

And he did. Albert and I did all the work. What Billy Bob did was shoot his pistols, talk about Hickok, read dime novels, and chase gals. That seemed like a pretty good career to me.

But there wasn't any use arguing. Billy Bob would just leave me somewhere high and dry. And the truth of the matter was, I didn't want to leave Albert and Rot Toe. Them and that wagon, scary as it could be sometimes, were all the home I knew.

I got the posters, a hammer and some tacks, and started up the street.

When we came to town, we always went about getting the sheriff's permission for our show, if we could. If we couldn't we pulled the Magic Wagon outside the town sign where his star didn't count and went ahead with it.

Course, some sheriffs didn't care for that, and they'd come out and run us off, a sign or no sign. I hated it when we had to spend a few days in jail. It just made Billy Bob all that harder to get along with. He'd blame me for too much starch in his long johns, go around frowning and kicking things, yelling at Albert and hitting Rot Toe with sticks until he got all the meanness out of him, or enough of it anyway. He was too full of it to ever get empty.

But most sheriffs were cooperative, and if they hesitated, Billy Bob could turn on the butter when he wanted to, and talk most of them into it. A sheriff is just like any other fella, in spite of what you might think. He likes a bit of a change now and then, and our show was better than spending his afternoons and early evenings with his heels on his desk, or going over to the saloon to pistol-whip a bunch of drunks into a stupor. Our shows had the added advantage of entertainment before the pistol-whipping, as most of the drunks would show up to see our acts and get looped as usual, only on our Cure-All if they didn't remember a pocket flask of their own. This being the case, the sheriff could watch our little act, then beat the drunks over the head with his gun barrel instead of having to make a special trip on over to the saloon.

So it was with only a few misgivings that I made my way over to the sheriff's office.

When I found it, the door was locked and there was a messy written sign tacked to it:

I AINT HERE NOW AND AINT GONNA BE
TILL SATERDEE. HOLD ALL KILLINS AND
SICH TILL I GIT BAK OR LOK YER OWNSEF
UP. RILEE OVER TO THE SALOON HAS THE
KEE.

I could just imagine that lawman spit-wetting his pencil and snickering over that sign as he wrote it. As Albert told me time and again, "You can say what you wants about them sheriffs, but them that I've known of has mostly got a sense of humor."

It also brought to mind a story Albert told me once about this sheriff down San Antone-way that could tell a joke better than you ever heard. Way Albert told it, he could get a fella laughing all the way out of the jail, up the gallows steps, and still cackling till the rope cut him off. Which is understandable at that point.

But Albert said this sheriff was good. He was not only a joker, he was a prankster. When things got slow around the jail and he had a prisoner, one of his favorite things was to unlock the cage while the fella was asleep, sneak in and put matches between his toes, light them, and sneak out.

You can imagine the chuckles this sheriff got when the matches reached the meat and that fella came leaping off his bunk and went rain dancing around his cell.

But in spite of this sense of humor, or maybe you could say because of it, this sheriff's story ended kind of tragic. As Albert pointed out, there's always someone out there lacking a sense of humor, and as fate would have it, the sheriff I'm telling you about got just such a stick in the mud in his jail.

This stick in the mud was known as a sour customer anyway, and what he was in jail for didn't liven his personality any. He'd gone on a rampage killing his wife, mother-in-law, and as good an old blue mule as ever pulled a plow. Can't recall what the wife's and mother-in-law's names were, but the mule was called Old Jesse.

What got this farmer riled in the first place, as is often the case with a man, was his mother-in-law. She lived with them, and didn't have any table manners to speak of. She was kind of elderly, and bad about breaking wind at the supper table. Maybe she could help it, maybe she couldn't. But it seemed to this farmer that she didn't give it a passing thought, and did it mostly to irritate him, never so much as offering up an excuse me, or asking how the most recent one compared to the last. It wasn't nothing to her, and he felt certain she was laughing behind her hand at him cause she knew it got on his nerves and spoiled his appetite.

Well, one evening, things simmered to a head. They were sitting at the table, spooning some ham and gravy and sweet taters, or whatever, and what does this old lady do but cut loose with a honker that would have shamed a pack mule. This farmer claimed it was so powerful the kitchen curtains billowed, but I think either the farmer or Albert exaggerated a little there. Anyway, she went on to choose this time to finally comment on it, and it wasn't a thing that charmed him in the least.

"Catch that one and paint it green," she said, and giggled.

The man went beside himself, snatched up the kindling axe and dove for her. As fate would have it, his wife got in the way and tried to stop things. All she got for her trouble was a new part in her hair, about six inches deep. Then the mother-in-law bit the hatchet. And if that wasn't enough, the farmer turned drunk-Injun mad, went out to the lot, and axed the mule.

This mule killing was quite a blow to the community. Old Jesse had been borrowed by every farmer in the county, and it was said that he was such a good plower lines weren't needed. Didn't even have to say gee or haw. You just took hold of the plow handles and Old Jesse did the rest without so much as lathering up.

Yep, that mule's fame was spread far and wide. Later on they had a funeral for him, and Albert said he heard a right smart number of folks showed up to attend the laying away services and do some gospel singing.

Well, Mule Slayer, as he came to be known, was brought to jail, and while they were waiting on trial, things got slow around the cell, and this sheriff with the sense of humor decided to liven things up with his famous hot-foot routine.

So, one afternoon, Mule Slayer was all stretched out on his bunk, catching a few winks, digesting his jail dinner, when the sheriff snuck into his cell, put matches between the fella's toes, lit them, and snuck out.

When the matches burned down to Mule Slayer's foot, he let out a roar, hit the floor two-stepping and barn dancing around the cell.

The sheriff thought this was real funny, and he had to lean up against the bars so he wouldn't fall down laughing. He started clapping his hands and singing one of those dosi-do-grab-your-partner songs, and that's just what Mule Slayer did. He promenaded on around there and shot a hand through the bars and got the sheriff by the goozel, reached the gun out of the old boy's holster, and took the keys off of him.

Damned if Mule Slayer wasn't suddenly in a joking mood himself. He put the sheriff on the bunk, strapped him down with pieces of the sheriff's gun belt and suspenders, and set the bed on fire, and as it was stuffed with feather ticking, it lit up real good. Albert said folks claimed later they could see smoke, hear that sheriff screaming and Mule Slayer laughing for a half mile or better, but I sort of doubt that myself.

When the townsfolks got there, they beat out the sheriff with a couple of brooms and throwed water on him, but it was too late. There wasn't enough left of him or the feathers to sweep up in a dust pan. Most of the old boy was soot on the walls. Even his badge had hotted up considerable. It had melted into a tiny ball, fallen between the bed springs, and rolled off into the corner.

They hauled Mule Slayer off to a place that wasn't burned up and smelled like a community barbecue, and made him a makeshift jail till things could get repaired at the real place, or until a trial came around.

Now Mule Slayer had caught a sense of humor, and he had caught it good. He laughed through the night, and the shed they had him in practically rocked with it.

This went on for several days, and it got so tiresome to the townsfolks, who could hardly sleep at night for the noise, that the gallows got built in no time, even though they had to rip the front porch off the general store to have enough lumber to get it done in a hurry.

A judge was appointed quickly, and the fella was tried, legal-like, though he laughed through the proceedings, which were cut down to five minutes, and he was sentenced to hang. Before they went out to do that, a prayer was said for Old Jesse.

Mule Slayer was still laughing when they put the rope around his neck, and would have kept on laughing if someone in the crowd hadn't yelled something about the sorry thing he'd done to that good mule.

This hit a note with Mule Slayer and he stopped laughing. He looked heavenward and said a few repentive words concerning the sad and unnecessary death of Old Jesse, and how he should have just stuck to his big-mouthed wife and stomach-ailed mother-in-law. Which was the general sentiment of the crowd.

In the process of saying these words about Jesse, he led on up to the jail and what happened there, and darned if he didn't get tickled all over again. This time he was giving all the details on the sheriff burning, which he hadn't before. He told how it was a lucky thing the suspenders and gun belt didn't burn up quicklike, freeing the sheriff, and he gave a real good description with mouth noises that perfectly imitated the sound of fire catching to feathers, bed springs squeaking, and the sheriff yelling. He then went on to the description of the sheriff wiggling around and sputtering like fat pork in a frying pan, and if Albert is to be believed, Mule Slayer was just getting to the good, nasty part when the eager beaver at the switch jerked the lever and dropped that kidder, midstory, through the hole.

There was darn near a riot.

Albert said that it was fair to say some good came out of the entire mess, and you might say the sheriff's fun-loving spirit had been passed onto Mule Slayer. One can only hope that same spirit, like a dose of pox, latched onto the fellow at the gallows switch, so next time there's a story going he ain't interested in, but others are, he'll have the good manners to hold out till the tale is told before giving his charge a hemp necktie.

• • •

With the sheriff gone, the permission problem was out of the way too, so I nailed one of my posters over his sign and went on down the street asking folks if I could do the same in their stores. I even went down to the church and tacked one on the door there, just in case the preacher wanted to come.

We liked to save a little space at the first of our show for a preacher, just in case he had a hankering to talk on the sins of the world and such, and how we were all going to hell in a handbasket.

Time he was finished the crowd's eyes would be glazed over good, like a horse that's fixing to die on you, and they'd be darn near ready for most anything but another dose of Get Jesus Saltz.

Another thing, those preachers were good for three, maybe four bottles of Cure-All. Reckon they liked to have that much on hand in case of snake bite, as they had to travel pretty far out in the country sometimes to find the sinners that are minding their own damned business and not putting anything in the offering plate. And all those dinners and suppers preachers ate, as they have a way of showing up at meal time, were bound to upset their stomachs now and then. And a good slug of Cure-All after a meal of fried chicken, flour gravy, mashed potatoes, buttered biscuits, and two slices of fresh apple pie with cream on top were just the thing to set a belly straight.

Finally I came to the saloon and hesitated outside the bat wings, sort of getting the lay of the land. Sometimes a bartender will consider me too young to be in a place and will throw me out. But most of them could care less if I was twelve years old, armed and dangerous, long as I was white and had the price of a beer. I was trying to decide which kind of place this was.

Like most saloons it smelled like beer, sweat and cigar smoke. I thought it over, decided the odds were on my side, put a hand on the bat wings, and went inside.

For early morning, there was a right smart crowd in there. I figured with the sheriff gone the owner had most likely kept the place open all night, grubbing for the extra drunk dollars.

There was a farmer and a bony saloon gal at one table, and they were entwined tight as a couple pieces of cheap rope. They had their eyes closed to show how in dreamy wonder they were of each other's company, and since it was as hot as a bitch dog in heat in there, they had a sheen of oily sweat on their faces thick as a swath of hot lard. I reckoned that farmer's wife thought he was in town buying seed, not sowing it.

At another table a fellow lay face down, and the only thing holding him up was his face and the edge of his butt in the chair. His arms hung by his sides like limp horse tails, and the one nostril that wasn't mashed into the table was making a noise like a busted bagpipe.

At a table behind him were two other fellas. One of them was about my age, and duded up. He had on a tall sky blue hat and his brown hair grew long out from beneath it. A red neckerchief was tied loosely around his neck, and he wore a fringed cotton shirt all the colors of the rainbow. The boots that stuck out of his cuffed jeans were so bright and new-looking I wouldn't been surprised if they'd mooed at me.

He was holding a dime novel close to a low-lit lamp at his table, moving his lips over the words. I could have saved his lips a lot of work. I could make out the title of what he was reading, *Young Wild West and the Salted Mines, or The Double Game for a Million*, and I had read it. It was about five years old and it wasn't worth the match it would have taken to burn the sucker up.

Wasn't no use saying anything, though. Just my opinion. And it might have resulted in me being beat up by a little fella in a dude outfit. He had that same look Billy Bob gets when he's reading those things. It's somewhere between the one a man gets when he's having his first peek at a naked woman, or is getting pulled into a religious soul-saving fever. Either one makes for a dangerous time if interrupted or disagreed upon.

Sitting next to Blue Hat was a fiftyish man, thick around the middle, with bullwide shoulders, a black derby hat gone green, and a face that looked like lumpy gravy poured over peanuts. I figured he'd once had the pox. On his upper lip were a few stray hairs that he probably called a mustache, but they reminded me of the prickles around a porcupine's butt. The way his eyes were squinted, you got the impression he was bored and wanted to shoot someone, just anybody, no matter how small the cause.

And he had the equipment to do the shooting. In a half holster hooked at his middle, dangling like a metal Johnson in leather underwear, was a single action Colt's .41 short barrel. It was engraved with all manner of gee-gaws, and the grip was faded, yellow ivory.

You didn't see folks toting guns like that out in the open much anymore, but this fella looked as comfortable that way as a pig in slop.

I didn't look at him long, least he catch me staring and decide to end his boredom by seeing how close he could space six rounds in one of my eyeballs.

I went over to the bar. The bartender was behind it, sweeping furiously with a broom. Dust was whipping up and around him like a twister, but if he was doing any good I couldn't tell it. It all settled down behind him as he swept forward.

He was skinny and wore an apron with more spots on it than a pinto horse. Most of the spots were beer, but there were some real interesting, crusty ones that I couldn't make out. His hair was the thing that had my most attention, however. It was slickered down with what looked like axle grease, and he was wearing some foo-foo water that made me dizzy before I got to him.

Behind him on the wall, just above the flyblown mirror, was a sign that read: NO GUNS ALLOWED IN HERE, and just under that: WE DON'T SERVE NIGGERS, FREED OR OTHERWISE.

I would have bet they backed up the bottom sign, but I didn't see anyone rushing to throw the fella with the derby and the pistol out in the street.

I sat down on a stool and the bartender came over. When he got up close I could smell something familiar and unpleasant underneath all that foo-foo water. I saw too, that a couple of big blue-bottle flies had lit in his hair. They were buzzing and beating their wings something furious, as they were stuck there like dog hairs to molasses.

"What's fer ya?" the bartender said, leaning over the bar at me. I could smell peppermint candy on his breath, but it wasn't enough to overpower the foo-foo water and what was underneath it. I couldn't help but lean back on my stool.

Earlier, I'd thought I might buy a beer without a fight, but at that moment, I wasn't so sure my belly could handle it. The bartender's aromas were about to smother me.

"Nothing for me, thank you," I said. "I just come by to ask a favor." I went through my rigamarole about the poster, and was just about to hand him one to look over, when out of the back of the saloon came this stocky man with a thatch of brown hair on his head that looked like a little dead animal. He had a determined stride, like a miner on his way to a free lunch. He walked right up to the bartender and slapped him a lick on the head with the flat of his hand. The blow was loud enough to be mistaken for a rifle shot. I think the passed-out drunk even flinched a bit. I know the farmer and his gal came untwined for a moment, probably thinking the wife had showed up mad with a Winchester. Behind me and to the left, I heard the man with the derby laugh. I knew it was him without even turning to look. I figured the kid hadn't looked up from his dime novel.

I got back on my stool, because I'd already started for the door, and put my bottom on it lightly, just in case I need to run after all. I leaned over the bar to look for the bartender. He was stretched out on the floor, face down, flat as a rug. The man who had slapped him was looking at his hand. His face was crunched up and a low moan came out from between his lips. There was some of the little man's hair slickum on his hand and one of his flies — mashed now.

"Damned idiot," the stocky man growled, and he kicked down behind the bar. The skinny fella had only been playing dead, because now, like a big toad, he hopped to his feet and darted for the door. The stocky man sailed a half-full bottle of whisky after him, but his aim was off and slow, and the bottle went over the bat wings and into the street just as Skinny took a sharp left and disappeared. Way that apron had slapped around him as he ran brought to mind something, but right at that moment it wouldn't come to me.

"I told you not to slicker your hair down with that damned cow mess," the stocky man yelled after Skinny. He turned to me, gave me a kind of grin, then he bent down behind the bar and came up with a nasty-looking rag. He used it to wipe his hand off, saving the fly and the spot it was on for last. He thumped the fly with his forefinger down the length of the bar where it skidded in a puddle of beer and skipped like a stone to the floor. Then he used the rag on the spot and tossed it under the bar again. He sniffed his hand and frowned. He got a bottle of whisky and poured a smidgen on his palm, sniffed again, and looked pleasant. He put the bottle back and smiled at me. "What's fer ya?" It was exactly the same voice and words Skinny had used, and I realized then that Skinny had the same knack mockingbirds do, except with people. He could copy perfectly whatever he heard spoken.

"I take it he ain't the bartender?" I said.

"No, he ain't. He ain't nothing but an idiot-fella I let sweep up now and then for a few beers and peppermints, and he ain't worth them. He tries to pretend he's me from time to time, but he ain't supposed to do nothing but clean up some. God...can you imagine, combing your hair with cow pies?"

"Well, it ain't something I'd do," I said.

"I think it's them blue bottles he likes, thinks they're pretty. I've seen him looking at them in the mirror here. I don't know why I even let him come around."

"Some of us are just big-hearted and foolish," I said.

"Reckon that's the truth. And it don't get you nowhere, nowhere at all. There's such a thing as being too damned good. Kind of a curse to me. My mama's at fault. She used to say to me, 'Riley,' she called me Riley, 'you take a care for other folks now, you hear?' and I always have. Not that it's done good by me, no sir. I'd be rich if I wasn't always giving of myself and my money. That addle-brained bastard is just a waste of my time. He don't do nothing I don't have to do again."

"It is a burden," I said, "I can see that. What I was trying to do here, Mr. Riley —"

"Just Riley."

"Riley. Was find out about putting these posters up. One inside, one out. They've got to do with a medicine and magic show this afternoon and tonight."

"Just as long as it ain't a tent preaching poster. I don't allow them kind of posters in here. Makes business fall off. How old are you anyway, boy?"

"Seventeen...and a half?"

"Old enough. How about a beer on the house."

"I'd like that, Mr. Riley."

"Remember, just Riley." He reached under the bar and brought out a half-filled glass of beer and slapped it on the counter. It tasted lukewarm and it was as flat as Amarillo. I figured it was what a customer had left undrunk and Riley had saved it for just such an occasion, being so big-hearted and neighborly like as he was. I didn't drink no more of it, just sat there and tried to look fat, dumb, and happy. The first part was the toughest, as I wasn't a hundred and forty pounds soaking wet with rocks in my pockets.

About that time I heard a chair scrape. I looked over to see Derby getting up and Blue Hat following, bending the dime novel into his back pocket. As they walked out, Derby grinned at the drunk and kicked the fella's chair out from under him. The drunk smashed to the floor and lay there with his face down and his butt up, a little stream of red running out of his nose. Derby and Blue Hat both laughed, and to get in on the act, Blue Hat kicked at the drunk's butt and sent him toppling on his side. The drunk lay there, bent up like half a doughnut, breathing hoarsely. One of his eyes half opened, then closed down quickly, like an old biddy lifting and lower the shade, casual like, for a peek at the neighbors.

"You need you some practice sitting in them chairs, don't you, you old souse?" Blue Hat said.

The drunk didn't say anything.

"You'd best answer when I talk to you," Blue Hat said, and he kicked the drunk in the belly.

The drunk made a gurgling sound and threw up some of what made him a drunk.

"Now you answer me," Blue Hat said in that sour, whining voice of his, hitching up his pants at the same time. "You don't sit in chairs so good, do you?"

"No sir," the drunk said, and more vomit bubbled out of his mouth.

"Filthy old fool," Blue Hat said. "You puke on me and I'll kill you." He looked over at Derby to see if he was doing his meanness right. He must have been. Derby was grinning some tobacco-stained teeth at him.

Blue Hat's head bobbed in my direction. "What you looking at? You need something?"

"Not a thing," I said and turned back to the bar. I put my hand around the glass of beer just to have something to do. The beer in the glass wobbled from side to side.

Riley suddenly took an urge to wipe the bar. He grabbed the nasty rag out from beneath it and worked on down to the far end, quicklike. I watched Derby and Blue Hat in the mirror, trying to look like I was just staring into space.

"You keep it that way," Blue Hat said.

Derby smiled at me, and there was something in that smile that chilled me to the bone. If Blue Hat had been carrying a gun I'd probably have felt the same way about him.

They laughed and went out.

When I was sure they were gone, I went over and helped the drunk back into his chair. By the time his head touched the table again, he was out. I used a snot rag I had to wipe his mouth and nose, and left it on the table in case he wanted it when he woke up. The two lovers opened their eyes to peep at me, then closed up again. I went back to the bar and took my seat. My hands were still shaking so I put them around the beer glass. I felt sort of weak.

"Who were those knee slappers?" I said to Riley, trying to sound a lot braver than I felt. "Father and son?"

"Dog and flea," Riley said softly, and he glanced toward the door when he said it. "That there fella in the derby hat," he added, picking up one of my posters and pointing to the part about Billy Bob and his expert pistol shooting, "he'd most likely make your man look like a blind nigger with a slingshot."

"Billy Bob is the best shot I've ever seen," I said. And that was the truth. I didn't like him any, but he could shoot. I'd seen him challenged many times, and no one came close. He could toss nickels in the air and hit them dead center. He could hold a mirror in one hand, lay his pistol over his shoulder, and shoot a playing card in half edgewise. Even on his bad nights he was better than anyone else.

"Well, you ain't seen that fella bang at it," Riley said. "Ain't no slouch on the fast draw neither. Maybe you've heard of him? That there was Texas Jack Wentworth."

Texas Jack. I'd heard of him all right. Even read about him in some of Billy Bob's dime novels. He wasn't as well known as Wild Bill Hickok, Buffalo Bill, and some others, but he did have a rep as a crackerjack of sorts.

Of course, now that I'd seen him, I was a mite disappointed. The dime novels painted him out to be a tall Greek god. Hell, he wasn't even tall. And that face of his wasn't recent. That was a mug he'd carried with him all his life, and those smallpox lumps weren't new either. Worse than that, he wasn't nothing but a bully and had a pet bully he took around with him. It was downright disappointing. At least Billy Bob looked like the characters in the books, even if there wasn't one written about him.

But it was pretty much on record that Jack had once outshot Doc Carver, and at one time Carver was the finest shot in the world. With a Winchester 73, Carver broke five-and-a-half thousand out of six thousand glass balls tossed in the air, and he did it in a seven and a half hour stretch. I heard too that he let some of his opponents use shotguns, and he used that Winchester, and still showed them up. So if Jack beat them like the stories went, even if Doc Carver was at the end of his career, he did some good shooting. That into consideration and there being a story that he'd once backed down Wild Bill Hickok, it was fair to say that Riley was right when he said the man wasn't no slouch.

"That Jack is a corker," Riley went on, suddenly talking as if the man were his brother. "I know all about him and I've heard tell more. He grew up around here before he went off and got famous, became an Injun fighter and buddy to John Wesley Hardin. Not that he wasn't known around here when he was your age. But it wasn't nothing special like later, he just shot a couple of nigger farm hands over some peach wine. Seems like maybe he shot his uncle too, but it's been a while since I heard that, and it could have been a cousin or something.

"Anyway, he went off and was wrote about in them dime novels. Then, about five years ago, a winter colder than the far side of a widow's bed, I was in here polishing the fly tracks off the glasses, when in walks this sombreroed greaser, big as you please. Strolled up to the bar like he was a white man, sitted himself on a stool, about where you're sitting I think, and called to me for a whisky.

"Well, you can bet I didn't hop to it, that's what I'm trying to tell you. I don't cotton to niggers and greasers and I sure don't cotton to them in my place trying to order me around like common help. I told him we didn't serve niggers, even if they was Mexican niggers.

"He got uppity on me and argued, then he jumped off the stool and pulled a pistol out from under his coat. And I'll tell you, for a Mex he was fast. I was standing here tonguing my teeth, waiting to hit hell's hot water, when a loud voice from the rear of the place yelled, 'Hey, Peppergut!'

"That Mex turned, bringing his gun around, and there was Jack, though we didn't know it was him at the time. He'd come in and nobody had recognized him. It was winter, you see, and he was bundled up in coats and shirts and had on this derby. And it had been some years.

"Well, I was thinking that this fella—Jack, but I didn't know it then—was going to get his big mouth shot off, and to be honest, that was all right by me, cause that meant I wasn't going to get bucked off my ride, you see. But before I could hit the floor and crawl off, Jack drew.

"Let me tell you, sonny, that was the prettiest draw I've ever seen, especially with it coming out from under all them coats. Ever seen a rattler strike, boy? It's something if you're not on the biting end of it. A rattler can coil, come off the ground and throw its head back, pop them fangs and hit you faster than you can blink. Well, this was even faster, I swear.

"Before that Mex could level his pistol, Jack fired. His shot hit the Mex solid between the eyes, and that peppergut folded up like a pair of fresh-washed long johns and hit the floor. Wasn't nothing left for him but to be hauled off to the trash ditch on the other side of town. I kept the Mex's pistol."

Riley reached under the bar and came up with it. It was a big, old, heavy .44.

"Ever since that night, Jack's had free drinks on me and run of the place. And that kid in the blue hat is Noel Reasoner. He was working for me at the time, sweeping up the back there. He saw the whole thing. He was always reading them dime novels, you know, and had just read one with Jack in it. And lo and behold, the top dog his ownself shows up and blows a spick's brains out right in front of him. Kid loved it. He's been following Jack around ever since, learning to shoot from him, and I hear he ain't even half bad."

"That's why Jack can tote a gun in here? He saved your life?"

"Jack could tote an elephant in here if he wanted," Riley said. "I ain't no fool. I just let him be. Homer, that's the sheriff, he don't bother him none neither, and we don't fault Homer none for it. He was something in his time, best sheriff in these parts. He tracked down and arrested Wild Bill Longley single-handed once. But now he's seventy and he and Jack get along good. And the town, they don't care that Jack totes a gun when they can't. He's sort of a living legend. He's in them dime novels and all. I reckon he's deserving of some special privileges."

From what I'd seen, he was deserving of about six feet of dirt on a box with him in it, but I wasn't the one who was going to say anything about it. I didn't reckon I was ready for my six feet of dirt, and if I wanted to stay out from under it, I reckoned the best thing for me to do was not run my mouth. Besides, I might not even get the six feet of dirt. They might treat me like they did that Mexican fella. Toss me in the garbage ditch outside of town.

I put up a couple of posters and smiled my way out of there, and when I came out I saw the idiot sitting on the boardwalk drinking from the bottle Riley had throwed at him. He looked pretty lonely sitting there. Even his flies had flown off. He glanced up at me and grinned. I grinned back and got four bits out of my pocket. It was a lot of money, but I felt like him getting slapped and kicked was sort of my fault.

"Here," I said, "take this and go buy yourself some peppermints."

He took the money, looked at it in the palm of his hand, then smiled at me. He got up and walked off.

I watched him go down the boardwalk toward the general store, apron flapping around him, the whisky bottle dangling from one hand like a big, fat finger. It struck me then what he reminded me of. The crazy Onin fella I had found in the ditch that winter.

I went the other way, put up some more posters, then went back to the Magic Wagon. Billy Bob was still sleeping.

Chapter Four

The preacher got there first, which is often the case, and we told him he could make a little talk when the crowd was big enough, but we'd appreciate it if he didn't try to get folks into a round of gospel singing.

We had everything set up. The mules had been pulled off the wagon, fed and watered, and were tied out next to the woods. We had the clearing fixed up for Billy Bob's shooting show, and we had the ring built for Rot Toe to wrestle in. The ring was six tall poles buried deep in the ground and a wide-hole netting pulled around it and over the top. This way, Rot Toe couldn't get out and scare folks, and the fellas he wrestled with couldn't get away. It kept Rot Toe from doing another thing which wasn't popular with the crowd, and that was throwing his wrestling partners at them. Albert said that back when they first got Rot Toe and come up with the wrestling bit, they used a common roped-in ring, but Rot Toe threw his partners out pretty regularlike. This kept Albert busy picking up folks and brushing them off, and when men who had planned to wrestle the ape saw two-hundred pound men, and sometimes bigger, flying through the air and smashing against the ground right smart, it made them look off in other directions and push their two-bits wrestling fee deeper into their pockets.

We had the side of the wagon facing the woods unhinged at the top and pulled down with supports under it to make a stage. Where the wall had been we pulled a blanket curtain across to keep Billy Bob and the stuff in the wagon hid. That way he could make his entrance out from behind the blanket. He just loved that kind of thing, and I have to admit, when he was duded up and ready to give a show, there was something almost magic about him, and even more so since we'd gotten that body in the box. He'd have probably done good in something like Buffalo Bill's Wild West Show, and I wished from time to time that he'd run off and join it.

Finally enough crowd got there for the preacher to preach to, and by the time he finished others had showed up and it looked as if we were going to have quite a gathering. The thing now was to entertain them good, then come on with the Cure-All and hope to sell a couple cases at the worst.

I looked out at the crowd to see if Texas Jack was out there, but didn't see him, which gave me some relief. I figured if Jack showed and saw Billy Bob's shooting, he'd want to shoot too, and in the end Billy Bob would find out he was the fella out of some of his dime novels, the one who was supposed to have backed down his hero, Wild Bill Hickok, and that could mean a killing. Billy Bob was just looking for an excuse to use those guns of his, and defending the honor of Wild Bill would be just the thing.

When the crowd was good-sized, Albert gave me the high sign and I climbed up on the stage. I had on my city-slicker suit with the derby and I felt about as natural as a pig in boots, but it comforted people to see a boy dressed up.

"Ladies and gentlemen," I said, "tonight, we got a special treat for you. We're going to show you some shooting the likes of which you've never seen. We're going to show you some magic. We're going to let any man who thinks he's man enough to wrestle with Rot Toe, the chimpanzee from Africa. And there's even more. But to introduce the events and demonstrate the manly art of six guns and bullets, I give you our star, the one, and the only, Billy Bob Daniels."

Nobody clapped. They were waiting to see if there was anything to clap about.

A moment later Billy Bob stepped out from behind the curtain and the clapping began.

I'll tell you, he did look good. He had something about him, and it was stronger and richer than ever before. He was wearing a wide-brimmed, tan hat with a band of rattlesnake hide around it, and his shirt and pants were fringed buckskins the color of butternut, and the buttons on his shirt were ivory-colored bone. Around his waist was a blood-red sash and there was a big Bowie knife stuck in the left side of it, and stuffed more to the front were his revolvers, butts out.

His revolvers were just like the ones Hickok's corpse had. Cartridge converted Colt 60's. They were sightless, so as not to snag on the draw, and the gun metal was almost blue. The grips were magnolia white.

On his feet were moccasin-styled boots with heels, which put another two inches on his height. The boots were the same color as his hat and they had fancy bead and quill work that started at the top and ran down to the toe point.

Billy Bob held up his hand and the clapping stopped. He walked out to the edge of the stage, took a moment to look over the crowd and smile. It was the smile he used when he was winning over the gals.

"My name is Billy Bob Daniels," he said. "I am the son of Wild Bill Hickok."

He let that soak in before he went on.

"Yes, I know what you're thinking. You're thinking I'm saying that for effect, that it's part of the act. But the truth is I am James Butler Hickok's illegitimate son. My mother was a fallen woman of Deadwood, and that is where I was conceived, shortly before that coward Jack McCall snuck up behind Wild Bill and shot him through the back of the head. Even so, my father's hand, out of pure reflex alone, had half drawn his pistol before he fell forward on his cards. Aces and eights, ladies and gentlemen. The cards that from that day forth have been known as the dead man's hand.

"Well, my mother didn't want me. That's the sad truth. I was given up to a family named Daniels and raised by them and it wasn't until I was a grown man that I knew the truth, knew that I was actually a Hickok."

Billy Bob had a way of getting a little trill in his throat when he talked about Hickok, and I'll tell you, it was darn near enough to make you believe that Hickok was his papa, even if like me, you knew it wasn't so. Or reckoned it wasn't so. Albert told me it wasn't true, and that was enough for me.

"When we were in Deadwood some time ago," Billy Bob said, "I met a kindly old medicine man, and he told me a secret. He told me this because he recognized me as the son of Wild Bill. He said he knew it instantly. He came forward, and you know what he told me? He told me the body of Wild Bill was not in its grave. That's correct, ladies and gentlemen, not in his grave. This old Indian whose life my father had saved on countless occasions, had stolen it, out of respect, mind you, and with herbs and spices known only to Indians, he had petrified the body and kept it in a cave where he bowed down before it twice a day to give thanks to Wild Bill for having saved his life.

"But you know what he did? He took me to that body, and because I'm Wild Bill's son, he gave it to me. And, ladies and gentlemen, that body is here today for you to see."

Albert had slipped into the back of the wagon, and now he came out from behind the curtain rolling the box on a hand truck, and when he stopped dead center of the stage, Billy Bob stepped over, grabbed the lid, and swung it back.

Hickok's body had been set up so that his arms were lifted and the revolver barrels were resting on what was left of his shoulders, and when the lid came off, the arms fell forward, locked on the hinges Billy Bob had built into the elbows, and two wires attached to the back of the box and the revolver hammers, grew taut and the hammers cocked. That sudden movement of the arms, those hammers cocking loudly, always made the crowd jump back and there was usually at least one woman in the crowd that would squeal. This time darn near everybody jumped and squealed. I just loved that part.

When the crowd settled down, Billy Bob said, "Ladies and gentlemen, I present to you Wild Bill Hickok, preserved and holding the very revolvers that sent many a man to hell on his shadow."

Billy Bob used his finger to point out the hole in Hickok's head where McCall's bullet had come out, then backtracked into a story about how Hickok had saved the medicine man's life, and how when the Indian preserved the body he blessed it. Well, it was a good story and all, but it wasn't the truth. I remembered how we came by that box clear as if it were yesterday, and the only thing about Billy Bob's story was right was that there had been an Indian medicine man, and it happened in Deadwood. Or at least it got started there.

• • •

It was a rainy night in Deadwood and things had not gone well. Earlier that day we had given the show, but it was raining then too, and hardly nobody came, and them that did were soon run off by the rain, except for a couple of drunks, and Billy Bob nearly got in a fight with them. From then on Billy Bob's mood went from sour to mean. I think it had something to do with him expecting more from Deadwood, as it was the death place of his hero. But even the graveyard where Wild Bill was buried seemed to disappoint Billy Bob. I reckon he thought standing near the grave would be a spiritual experience or something, but I think all he got out of it was what me and Albert got out of it, and that was wet and cold.

So it was night and we had pulled out to the edge of Deadwood and were about to throw up a windblind for the mules and get bedded down, when this string-bean fellow in a black-and-orange check suit wearing a derby hat showed up. He got off his horse and came smiling up to us, the rain running off his derby like a waterfall.

I recognized him on account of that suit. He had been at the show that day, but like the others, the rain had run him off. I remembered that he had bad teeth, except for the front two. They were so big and thick-looking you could have tied either one of them on a stick and used it for a hoe.

"What's it we can do for you?" Billy Bob asked the fellow, and I seen his hand dip into his coat pocket, and for once I was glad Billy Bob had a pistol in there and knew how to use it. Something about the fellow in the checkerboard suit made me nervous.

"Mister," he says to Billy Bob, "I heard what you said about being the son of Wild Bill Hickok today, and I come to talk to you."

"That's about all you heard," Billy Bob said. "You left kind of early."

"Well sir, I wouldn't have, but the rain put a damper on the festivities."

"You didn't mind coming out here in it."

"No sir, I didn't. And that's because I got something to tell you, might be of interest."

"Well tell me, I'm wanting to get out of this rain."

"I know where the body of your father, Wild Bill Hickok, is."

"Well don't bandy it around you idiot, only everyone in these United States and the territories knows that. He's in Deadwood cemetery, you hollow-headed fool. I was up there today to look at his grave."

"No sir, he ain't there. But let me explain myself now. I'm Bob Chauncey, but folks call me Checkers on account of my suit." And he smiled real big.

Well now, I'll tell you. A man that wears the same suit enough to be named after it ain't high on my list of would-be partners. I ain't the best for cleanliness myself sometimes, but I don't live in the same suit neither. I have been known to put on a clean shirt once in a while. And I wasn't one to believe old Checkers washed out his coat and pants nightly and dried it. He wasn't the type. I think the fact that he had what my mama used to call an unsavory habit led me to figure him as something of a messy person. He was a nose picker, and about the best I've ever seen at it. He didn't do it like a lady will do, like she ain't really doing it but just scratching, and her finger will shoot in and scoop out the prize and she'll flick it away before you can say, "Hey, ain't that a booger?"

He didn't even do it like some men do, which is honest, but not impolite. They'll turn sort of to the side and get in there after it in a businesslike manner, but you didn't actually have to witness the work or what come of it.

No, Checkers Chauncey, who I think of as Nose Picker Chauncey, must have once been a miner or a mule whacker, as they're the nastiest, and the most mannerless creatures on earth. There ain't a thing they won't do in front of man, child, or lady. They just don't give a damn. Chauncey went about his digging front-on and open, using his finger so hard it rose a mound on his nostrils, like a busy groundhog throwing up dirt. And when he got what he was looking for, he always held it in front of him just to see, I guess, if he'd accidently found something other than what he expected, and when he thumped it away you had to be kind of fast on your feet, because he didn't care who or what it stuck to.

"Well, Checkers, if you think you can tell me where he is," Billy Bob said, "I'm all ears, and watch where you're thumping them things, will you?"

"Well, he ain't in no cemetery. That sign on his grave is just to fool folks. He used to be up there, but he ain't now. Few years ago they moved the cemetery and he got dug up. They were expanding the town, you see, needed the room.

Didn't want a bunch of rots and bloaters in the middle of the main street. So when they dug old Bill up, they opened his box and found he was in pretty good shape for a dead man. Had petrified like an old tree. If you could have tore his arm off, it would have been hard enough I reckon to beat a good-sized pig to death."

"How come you know all this, Checkers?" Billy Bob asked.

"I was there when they dug him up. Was just a kid here in Deadwood when he got his brains blowed out. Missed that, which grieves me, since it was history in the making. Had a job emptying out the spittoons, and Mann's number ten was next on my route, but I didn't get there soon enough."

"So you're saying you saw him dug up and the body was taken then?"

"Nope, ain't saying that. Not right then. They reburied Bill, but that night a couple of fellas I knowed came and dug him back up, and they sold him to an old Sioux medicine man for the whereabouts of a mine up in the hills, as there was considerable gold digging going on then."

"Sold Wild Bill Hickok to an Indian?" Billy Bob said.

"Yep. And he wasn't just any old Indian. Hickok had killed his oldest son in some shindig once, and he had vowed to get Hickok's body someday. Those two miners remembered that, and they knew he knew these hills like a chicken knows an egg, so they made a swap with him."

"My God," Billy Bob said, "that ain't white."

"This old Indian made him a box out of some sacred trees, and he put that body in it. He figured the spirits in the trees would keep Hickok's dead spirit from getting out and doing something to him. Hickok was so good with them pistols of his, lot of folks, especially Indians, thought he had some magic in him, or in those guns. That box was the Indian's way of holding that magic back, get me?"

"I get you, but you still ain't told me where the body is."

"This old Indian liked to open the box up a couple times a day, lift up his breechcloth and expose himself to old Bill's corpse."

"That's disgusting," Billy Bob said.

"Showing your privates like that is a kind of Indian joke. An insult."

"All right, enough about the damned savages and their jokes, where is this old Indian that has the body?"

"The old Indian don't have it no more."

Billy Bob was starting to fidget, and I thought any minute he was going to jerk out that pistol and start beating Nose Picker about the head and ears with it, which would have been all right with me. I could see this was leading to no good, and I was cold and wet and getting wetter. Albert was leaning against the wagon, watching and listening. He didn't look any happier than I felt.

"I swear you are the windiest gas bag I ever did see. If he ain't with the old Indian, then where is he?"

"With the old Indian's son. He's a medicine man too. You see, the old man died and the young fella sort of inherited Wild Bill. He's been living back East getting him a white education, but he had to come back on account of he got caught cheating somebody in Yankee land. He has the body now and wants to sell it, get him some seed money. Get out of the cave he's living in. Maybe go back East when things cool down on what he done."

"And what's your cut in all this, Checkers?" Billy Bob said.

Checkers smiled. I wished he hadn't. I didn't like them teeth. "Finders fee. Indian said he'd give me a cut of the money, and then there's just the plain, simple fact that I'd like to see a family brought back together again, even if one of them is dead."

"That's right touching of you," Billy Bob said.

"Always did have me a sentimental streak. It's a kind of sweetness that runs through me. You interested or not?"

"I'm interested. And Checkers?"

"Yeah?"

"You wouldn't lie to an ole Southern boy, would you?"

"No. I wouldn't. I'm partial to Southern boys, actually."

"I hope you are. How much this Indian wanting for the body, provided I see it and want it?"

"Twenty dollars."

"Twenty dollars!"

"That's right. And twenty for me taking you to it."

"Hell, man, ain't nobody got no forty dollars to be giving away."

"Well now, I figure since he's your pa, you'll want the body. And another thing, maybe an even more important thing, is you have that body and you're going to make a ton of money. I mean, you can't kid Checkers. You carry that old boy around with you and it's going to sell more of that watered-down liquor you call Cure-All. And that's going to make you lots of money, I know."

"When do I see the body?" Billy Bob asked.

"Has to be tonight."

"That's a mite hasty, ain't it, considering the weather?"

"I'm leaving the Hills tomorrow. Don't know if I'm coming back. Hell, for all I know, that Indian might have already cut loose of it. He was big to sell."

So there we were, it pitch black and raining bad enough to strangle a duck, and Billy Bob wanted to go into the Black Hills with a total stranger who couldn't stop picking his nose, and look at a rotting body in a box. A body that might, or might not be, Wild Bill Hickok. Then he'd probably buy that rascal with the wages he owed me and Albert.

Billy Bob put the wagon in storage, put our old mules in the livery, and rented us some horses, including one for Chauncey, and one mule for carrying the box out should he buy it, which seemed like a foregone conclusion to me. Provided there was a body in a box.

We put Rot Toe over to one of the whorehouses, and I told one of the fat ladies to take good care of him, and if anything happened to us, which was damn likely, he was partial to fruit and would touch a bite of meat now and then if that's all there was.

By the time we were all squared away it was pretty late and raining worse than ever. I just couldn't see any sense in this thing we were doing, but I reckon I can't complain too loudly, because there wasn't much sense in me either. I went along and I could have deserted right then and there, lit out and never had to look at Billy Bob again. But I didn't , and I like to think it wasn't so much a dose of the stupids as it was the fact that I didn't want to leave Albert. You see, I knew, for whatever reason, he was going to stick with Billy Bob. And Billy Bob was one of them kind that once he got his mind set on a thing, he was going to do it, and there wasn't no swaying him. Way he was acting, you'd think Wild Bill really was his pap.

Nose Picker worried me too. He was too eager to my way of thinking. Even twenty dollars and the cut of another twenty didn't seem worth what he was doing. I figured soon as we were up in the Hills, bunch of his cutthroat partners would come out of the rocks, kill us, steal the rented horses, and take everything we had on us, right down to our underwear, and them too if they were in the right sizes.

In spite of all this, Billy Bob wasn't a total fool. He had put pistols in both his buffalo-coat pockets and he had another little one in his belt. He fixed me up with a .38 Smith-and-Wesson and gave Albert a big .45. Chauncey didn't see any of this, as he waited outside the wagon while we got a few things, and him not knowing about the guns was at least some sort of comfort.

As we rode I could see from the way Albert was looking all around, one of his hands inside his coat near the .45, that he felt like I did. He was worried.

I kept my hand away from the Smith-and-Wesson because I was afraid of guns, and figured if it came down to me using it, I'd most likely try to pull it and end up shooting off my kneecap, or some other part of my body I was even more proud of.

Billy Bob, on the other hand, looked like he was on a picnic, or like he had just ridden out of one of them dime novels he liked to read. The rain didn't even bother him. He sat straight in the saddle, face forward. He was wearing a big, wide-brimmed, black hat, that buffalo coat, dark blue pants with a yellow military stripe, and black, fur-lined boots.

Chauncey slouched in the saddle, smiling to himself, singing some ditty or another, picking his nose all the while. I couldn't tell if he was naturally happy, stupid, or thinking on what he was going to do with his share of the clothes and such he was going to help steal from us later.

Whatever, there we were, right smack dab out in the middle of what used to be called Red Cloud's Big Open, and any minute I expected to get my brains blowed out by robbers in cahoots with Nose Picker Chauncey, or maybe by some Indians that didn't know, or didn't care, that we had won the Indian wars.

But none of that happened.

After we'd ridden for quite a few hours and I'd begun to feel like my butt had growed to the saddle, we came on a bad section of rocks and the trail narrowed. Lightning flashed, and when it did I seen at the top of the trail that there were a series of small caves, and those caves looked like open mouths begging us to step inside and get chewed.

When the lightning flashed again, Chauncey pointed at one of the caves, and we got the general idea which one it was, and that that was where the Indian lived.

We started along the narrow trail that led up there, and I could hear pebbles tumbling off the edge and down to the depths below. When the lightning flashed again, I looked down and wished I hadn't. If me and my horse went over, there wouldn't never be no way to sort out which of us was which.

Finally we come to a spot about halfway to the caves and stopped. Chauncey got down and had us do the same.

"We got to walk the rest of the way," Chauncey said, and he had to yell for us to understand him because the wind was whipping away his words. "We can leave our mounts here. Get the nigger to hold them."

Though it would have been smarter for Billy Bob to have left me holding the mules, since I didn't know slick mud from fresh honey, he went along with Chauncey, seeing how Albert was colored. He damn sure didn't want no white man to know he'd feel safer with a colored by his side instead of one of his own kind.

"Let's go then," Billy Bob said.

I handed Albert the rein to my horse.

"You watch yourself, hear?" Albert said.

"I will."

So the three of us, Chauncey, Billy Bob, and me, went up.

It was a rough walk and the higher it got the less there was to walk on. Rocks slid out from under our feet and cut at our legs and the gorge loomed just to our left, and when the lightning flashed it looked deep enough for you to fall all the way down to the pits of hell.

After the jumble of rocks we came to a clear spot and the cave. There was a torch just inside against the wall, lodged in some rocks, and Chauncey lit it, which was quite a chore as he had to take a finger out of his nose to hold the torch in one hand and the match in the other.

When the torch was lit, we went deeper inside the cave. Bats flapped above us, and their leavings were all over the floor and smelt right smart. I didn't like bats, no kind of way. They always looked to me like rats with wings, and I don't like rats either. Especially ones that can fly.

Finally it got lighter ahead of us, and we crunched through some old bones lying about, and Chauncey showed us that a lot of them were human. He said this cave had once belonged to a grizzly and that now and then some folks had come in and met him, and he hadn't been such a good host. I know I was glad when he lifted that torch and I didn't have to stare at those bones, particularly one skull with its entire right side crushed in, like a big paw had swatted it.

The light around the bend was from a campfire, and it was right cozy in there. There were a few handmade chairs, a bed, and a table, and over on the right-hand side of the wall, leaning up against it, was a rough-cut box with a lid on it.

But the thing that really got my attention was the young Indian. He wasn't all that young, I reckon. Maybe thirty-five. It's hard to tell with Indians. They seem to me to either age real fast or not at all.

He had on a dusty black suit with a yellowish shirt that was once white and he was wearing an Abraham Lincoln hat. He was a friendly looking fellow and he was smiling at us while he held one hand in his coat pocket.

I figured he had his hand on a pistol and was just smiling either out of habit, or to get us off guard. When he seen that Checkers was with us, he relaxed a mite and spoke.

"Checkers, my good comrade. I thought that I might not see you again. It was my suspicion that you had been caught for some nefarious deed, like horse thievery, but I see that this was not the case. And better yet, you have brought friends to cheer my fire."

"Why's he talk like that?" Billy Bob half whispered to Checkers.

"That damned education stuff," Checkers said. "But he's all right."

"Come," said the Indian, "please come and warm yourself by my meager fire. Take a load off your feet and your mind, and I will see to some liquid refreshment."

What he did for liquid refreshment was reach into his other pocket and take out a pint flask which he sat on a rock by the fire.

We got over near the fire and warmed our hands, but nobody sat yet.

The Indian found four cups and brought them over, then he poured us all a little splash from the bottle and we drank it.

"Please, please," he said pouring us some more. "Sit, please do sit. There is no need to stand on parade here. My home is your home. Or to take two lines from the opera *Clari, the Maid of Milan*: 'Mid pleasures and palaces though we may roam, be it ever so humble, there's no place like home; a charm from the skies seems to hallow us there, which sought through the world is ne'er met with elsewhere.'"

Billy Bob wasn't so quiet this time. "What in hell is he talking about?"

"Just more of that education stuff," Chauncey said. "An opry is where folks yell at each other to music."

"Ah, Checkers," said the Indian, "you have no heart. An opera is the heart, the soul, the very wing tips of a bird. It soars through the breast and mind and fills the soul."

"How about we do less soaring," Billy Bob said, "and talk about this body I come to look at."

"Yes," the Indian said, "the body of the Great White Warrior, the Pistoleer Prince of the Plains, the one and only, the indescribable Wild Bill Hickok."

"That's him," Billy Bob said.

"Now you remember that deal you made me about bringing a buyer here?" Checkers said to the Indian.

"It has been a month, my good friend. But I remember." The Indian smiled. "What if you had brought them here and I had sold the body?"

"Chance I took," Checkers said. "Besides, I didn't figure you'd sold it. You don't like going down into town so much."

The Indian opened his arms wide. "Isn't that polite? That is Mr. Checkers' way of saying that I am a wanted man in Deadwood."

"What for?" Billy Bob said. "I thought it was back East where you was wanted."

The Indian sighed. "There too. But I can hide better here. As for Deadwood, well, I'm wanted for a slight altercation with a young gentleman who had some rather foul comments about my ancestry. I was forced in a moment of passion, perhaps a moment fired by devil rum, to place the full length of a Bowie knife between his top two ribs, and therefore, let the soul fly out of him."

"What?" Billy Bob said, glancing at Checkers.

"He stabbed the sonofabitch to death," Checkers said.

"And I hope, dear friend," said the Indian, "that you have been better able to quiet your tongue on that matter below than you have here this night."

"You told them, you silly bastard," Checkers said. "I was just explaining."

"So you were, so you were," the Indian said.

The Indian and Checkers grinned at each other. The way they were doing it, I figured it was hurting their lips.

"Can we just get on with what I come here for?" Billy Bob said.

"Of course," said the Indian, "but first let me introduce myself. I'm Elijah Bigshield, Oglala medicine man, retired." He held out his hand.

Billy Bob's face worked to the left, then to the right. "I don't shake hands with niggers or Indians," he said.

"You don't say?" the Indian said.

"I do say. Now let's get on with it."

Checkers cleared his throat. "This here boy has got a special interest in the body. Hickok was his daddy. Some whore in Deadwood was his mother."

"You don't say?" Elijah Bigshield said, but the honey in his voice had gone considerably sour. "Isn't that nice. Why you even look like him, now that it is mentioned. 'As a little childe riding behind his father, said simply unto him, Father when you are dead, I shall ride in the Saddle.' Stefan Guazzo, *Civile Conversation*. And now that saddle has been passed to you, and you may ride in the tracks of Hickok the killer."

I was beginning to feel a mite uncomfortable, but Billy Bob didn't show a sign of it. "I don't want to hear no more of your education," he said. "An Indian or a nigger with an education ain't nothing more than a bird that can talk. It sounds like it knows something, but any fool knows it don't. It just mocks."

"I find you most unpleasant, sir," Elijah said.

"You're going to find me leaning over your ugly face, beating you upside the head with my fist, if you don't show me this body Checkers has been carping about. And there better be a body in that damn box, that's what I'm trying to tell you."

"Anything to please the young gentleman," Elijah said snidely. He walked over to the box and rubbed a hand against it. "I'm asking twenty dollars for it, sir."

We followed him over, with Checkers standing back a bit, and Elijah opened the lid. That was the first time I seen the body, and I knew in my heart that it was none other than who they said it was, Wild Bill Hickok.

"The body possesses magical properties, sir," Elijah said stepping to the side to let Billy Bob see. "Hickok's ability with his guns was most phenomenal. And he himself said on more than one occasion that his hands were guided by spirits."

"How come you know so much about it, you being an Indian?" Billy Bob asked.

"Even the mouse must learn the ways of the hawk if he wishes to survive. That body, sir, is so full of magic, that it is said that if you put it at the foot of your bed at night, Hickok's skill with the pistols will enter into you and allow you to shoot as fast and straight and true as this man-killer ever did."

"Is that a fact?" Billy Bob said. "Who's done it to know?"

"No one. My father told me this, and he was one to know. He tried to steal the magic from the corpse and put it in a pot, but the magic was too strong to be stolen. When he died, my father's soul joined those in the wood that surround the white man-killer."

"The spirits in the wood, huh?"

Elijah nodded. The firelight flickered across his copper face, and even in that silly suit and hat, he looked very, very Indian. The smile lines around his eyes and mouth had fallen off like dead leaves.

"That is correct. The spirits in the wood are old as the world, and they collect to them new spirits when they die, providing those spirits are worthy to become the protectors of the Oglala."

"You don't say?" Billy Bob sneered.

"Oh, I do say. It is the spirits in the wood that keep the black magic of Hickok inside him, lest it be passed onto the whites. The whites have enough magic, without the gun magic of Hickok."

"And why don't you, or why didn't your father, let Wild Bill's magic pass onto you Indians?"

"White man's magic. It cannot be used by Indians, and Indians don't want it. We have our own magic."

"Lot of good it's done you," Billy Bob said.

"That is quite correct, sir," Elijah said, "quite correct." But his voice had an edge to it, and I was beginning to get spooked. I looked at the body in the box and it seemed strangely alive. It wasn't that I expected it to get out of that box and walk or nothing. It was more like what that medicine man was saying about spirits and all, and there was something about that body, maybe the way the firelight glinted off the bone in those empty eye sockets, that made you think there was a powerful and ugly thing inside it. I somehow felt whatever spirits might have been in Hickok were bad. Maybe Hickok wasn't all bad his ownself, but those spirits were, and now they were all that was left of him. I felt better knowing he was between them boards full of Indian magic.

"You tell a good story, Indian," Billy Bob said, smiling one of his nasty smiles, "but it ain't nothing to me but spook talk."

Elijah smiled slowly, so slowly you could almost count his teeth one at a time as his lips folded back. "Yes, you white men certainly have it over us ignorant savages."

Billy Bob nodded to that. "How do I know this here is Wild Bill Hickok, and not just some drunk you've pickled?"

Elijah stepped forward, put a finger on the body's head. "Bend close and look at that hole. Is that not an exit wound from a bullet? Was not Wild Bill shot from behind and the bullet came out the front of his head?"

"That's so," Billy Bob said, leaning forward for a look. In spite of myself, I leaned too, but I couldn't look into those empty sockets. Billy Bob was what I was looking at, and his eyes seemed to have fallen out of his head and down those sockets like two marbles tumbling down mine shafts. His face tightened for a moment, and then suddenly he turned.

Elijah, after pointing out that bullet hole, had stepped back and pulled what was in his coat pocket out. A Bowie knife. And even as Billy Bob turned, and I turned with him, that knife came flying through the air. To this day I don't know how it missed Billy Bob. I couldn't believe he could move that fast. His left hand came out of his coat pocket, and it was full of Colt's 60. The Colt jumped and roared and Elijah's lips were parted by the bullet. The gun roared again, and this time the slug hit Elijah square between the eyes. The shots were so close together, they almost sounded like one.

Before Elijah hit the ground, Billy Bob flicked his wrist to the left and had Checkers covered. Checkers had one hand to his nose and the other inside his coat.

"Don't shoot me, fella," Checkers said. "I was trying to go for the Indian. I seen what he was about to do and I tried to go for him. I swear, it was the Indian I was after. It's just you're so blooming fast...Grief, but you just might be the son of old Wild Bill. That was the fastest damned draw I ever did see."

Slowly Checkers went ahead and brought his gun hand out. There was a little pistol in it. He lowered his arm down by his side and let it dangle.

"I swear," Checkers said, "I wouldn't throw in with no Indian against a white man."

"Put the gun up," Billy Bob said, "and see if he's dead."

Checkers did as he was told. While he did I smelt something burning, and glancing at the fire I seen it was Elijah's stovepipe hat. The first shot had knocked it off his head and it had rolled into the fire. It was just a black wisp now. Checkers bent over the body, then stood. "He's dead. Course he's dead. He's got two holes in his head. I could have told you that from over there."

Billy Bob turned to look at where the Bowie had gone. It was stuck just to the right of Hickok's head. Billy Bob reached and pulled it out of the wood, and the knife squeaked free of it like a mouse that had had its back stepped on. Billy Bob stuck it in the belt around his coat.

"Too bad he wasn't white," Billy Bob said. "Would have been my first kill. Hickok didn't count no Indians or niggers, and I don't aim to neither."

"Didn't count spicks neither," Checkers said.

"That's right," Billy Bob said, "no spicks neither."

Billy Bob reloaded his pistol and dipped it back into his left coat pocket.

"Checkers," he said, "you look that body over for money. He got anything you give it to me. I ain't so sure you didn't lead us up here to cheat and kill us, so you don't get nothing out of the deal, not even the twenty for the trip."

Checkers' face went red and he forgot to put his finger in his nose. "That ain't fair."

"Didn't say it was," Billy Bob said. "Don't feel like being fair right now."

"I brought you up here in the rain, it storming—"

"Shut up and do as I say," Billy Bob said. He opened and closed his hands above his coat pockets where the butts of his pistols showed.

Checkers moved his jaw back and forth a few times, then he bent to searching Elijah.

"Don't palm nothing," Billy Bob said. "I would find that disagreeable."

Checkers brought over a pocket watch, a derringer, and a little bag full of bones, dirt, and beads.

Billy Bob put the watch in his inside shirt pocket. "Indians are hell for trinkets," he said, "but what they need to know time for?" He poured what was in the bag into his hand and then back into the bag. "What's this?"

"His medicine bag," Checkers aid. "Has his powers in it."

"Did him a lot of good, didn't it?" Billy Bob said, and tossed it into the fire. He flung the derringer as far as he could to the back of the cave. "Whore's gun," he said. "That and tin horns."

Billy Bob put the lid on the box, and we went out of there, back down to where Albert waited, me and Checkers carrying the box with Wild Bill in it. It was pretty heavy.

I didn't tell Albert right then all that happened. I figured he knew a lot of the story from the way I looked at him, and I thought maybe he'd heard the shots, though later he said he hadn't. With the storm like it was, and us being deep inside the cave, he hadn't heard a thing.

We strapped the box on the side of the mule, and Billy Bob took to leading it behind his mount. Me and Checkers rode behind him, almost side by side, and behind us was Albert.

We'd gone a mile or so when the storm got so bad every little bit of the sky lit up with forks of blue-white lightning and the thunder roared like there was a cannon war going on.

About the time all this storm business got built up, Checkers made his play. Maybe he and the Indian had planned such a thing all along and it hadn't gone good. I don't know. Maybe Checkers planned to rob us after we had the body and the Indian's money, that way he could make double. And maybe he hadn't planned nothing at all and was just mad because he hadn't made his share like he thought he should.

Doesn't matter now. With Billy Bob in front of him, he had the perfect chance to do to him what Jack McCall had done to Hickok.

I seen him go for his gun, and I tried to yell, but with the thunder and lightning like it was, I didn't know if Billy Bob could hear me. But he did, or maybe he'd just been waiting for Checkers to make his play all along. Billy Bob swiveled on his critter, and as he did, I seen there was a smile on his face, like he was about to get a present he'd been waiting a long time for.

The way Billy Bob's hand moved was too fast to be real. I figured it was a trick of the lightning or something. One second his hand was on his knee and the next it was full of pistol and the pistol was cocked.

Only he didn't get to kill Checkers. The lightning did it. It was faster even than Billy Bob, and it reached down out of the sky and hit Checkers' little pistol and there was the sound like a giant whip cracking, then Checkers and his horse exploded and I was wearing some of him and some of his suit and some of his horse.

Billy Bob, with a wail, threw himself off his horse onto the ground and started pounding his hand against the ground, screaming. "I had him beat. My first white man. I had him beat," then he began to cry.

I just sort of sat there, dumbfounded, wearing Checkers, his suit, and his horse. Finally I got down off my horse, led him over a piece, got down on my knees, and threw up.

When I was able to get up, I looked over and seen Albert was helping Billy Bob to his feet. Billy Bob was saying over and over, "I had him beat. My first white man."

Albert helped Billy Bob over to his horse and put him in the saddle. He patted him on the knee. "There's just a whole bunch of white men, Mister Billy Bob. Don't you fret. There'll be others."

"I had him, Albert. I had him whipped fair and square, didn't I?"

"Couldn't have been no fairer or squarer," Albert said, like he was talking to a little kid.

"It ain't right. I had him beat."

"Plumb beat," Albert said.

"By the time Wild Bill was my age he'd done a lot of his killing already," Billy Bob said.

"Things were different then," Albert said. "Folks was more for killing in them times. Got up with it on their minds. They had more niggers to do their work, and there was lots of free time for shooting folks."

"I had him," Billy Bob said, shaking his head. "I had him."

Actually, I had a lot of him. I got a handkerchief and cleaned off what I could and got sick some more.

When I was feeling some better, I went over and stood with Albert and he put his arm around my shoulder. We looked at what was left of Nose Picker Chauncey and his horse. It wasn't much. Just a heap of bones, smoking meat, some saddle leather, and a hunk of checkered suit.

Maybe I should have felt some worse about old Checkers, but to tell it true, I couldn't work up a lot of enthusiasm for feeling bad. I figured after he killed Billy Bob he planned to finish off me and Albert, not knowing we had guns on us and seeing us as easy pickings, which I reckon I would have been. And besides, I just couldn't warm myself to a man that spent the largest part of his life with a finger up his nose, even if he did end up sadlike, being cooked with a horse and a checkered suit.

It seemed like it took forever to get out of the hills, what with the storm being like it was and Billy Bob sort of pouting along, stopping now and then to shake his fists at the heavens and to cuss God and the lightning, calling them some of the meanest, foulest names I've ever heard a mouth utter. The way that thunder rumbled and that lightning sizzled blue-white around Billy Bob, framing him now and then like a bright-colored picture, I half felt it was cussing and threatening him back.

By the middle of the next morning we got down out of the hills and back to Deadwood. The sun still hadn't come out.

We collected the wagon, the mules, and Rot Toe, who smelled mighty sweet from all them women petting on him, and we got out of town lickety-split, started heading Southwest, which was a direction that suited me fine.

We hadn't gone a day out of that storm when Billy Bob decided to fix up some cracked sideboards in the wagon.

He'd been putting it off for a month and there didn't seem any sense in it right then, but I think he did it to make light of what that medicine man had told him about them boards in Wild Bill's box being made out of sacred trees. He knew I'd told Albert the story, and he knew that Albert believed it, and I about half believed it, so he wanted to show us what fools we were.

Like I said, we'd gotten ahead of the rain for a while, and had all been sitting on top of the wagon, trying to get us some sun, and suddenly Billy Bob had us pull over.

Usually, any work to be done, me and Albert did it, but this time Billy Bob took it on himself. He dragged the box with Wild Bill outside the wagon, propped the body against it, knocked out those old sideboards he wanted to replace, and put in some boards from Wild Bill's box.

It took about half a day for him to get that done, as Billy Bob wasn't no joiner to speak of, and by the time he was finished and we were on our way, thunder was right behind us, rumbling loud, and when I turned to look back I got the willies, cause them dark storm clouds that were following us looked to have come together in the shape of Elijah's stovepipe hat.

That was the day that storm started pushing for us, and it stayed after us from then on.

A week or so later, we stopped in a little town to do our act, and Billy Bob had a joiner make a new box for Wild Bill. When that was done, he took the guns that were in Wild Bill's rotting sash out, cleaned them up, and put them in the corpse's bony hands, rigged up those hinges in the elbows and those wires that cocked the guns.

And that's the true story of how we came by that body in the box, not the one Billy Bob was telling the crowd about a noble red man giving it to him because he was Hickok's son.

I mean, his tale was a good story, all right, but it was nothing
more than a damned lie.

• • •

To get back to this time in Mud Creek, Billy Bob told his
story, then he went out to the clearing with everyone tagging along behind, and he did some shooting.

And I mean shooting. I want to witness that I hadn't never
seen him as good as he was that day. He split playing cards
edgewise, like always, but now he was doing it from farther
away. The same for when he held the mirror with one hand
and shot over his shoulder with the other. And he hit nickels
tossed in the air with either hand. Before he'd only done that
kind of shooting with his right hand.

To put it simply, the man could not miss.

He even went as far as to strike a match with a shot, and
I'd heard that was just an old wives' tale and couldn't be
done. But he done it, and neatly.

When next I looked out at the crowd, I seen Skinny had
joined us. He still had on his apron. He was eating from a
bag of peppermints, drooling it down his chin. His eyes
looked like a couple of dark holes. It was kind of good to see
the old boy.

Then I seen something that made me considerably less
happy.

Blue Hat and Texas Jack.

Chapter Five

The way those two were smiling, I knew there was going to be trouble. They might as well have been waving flags. Texas Jack was grinning like what Billy Bob was doing was the silliest and easiest thing in the world, and wasn't it a damned shame that all those people were oohing and aahing over him so much.

Blue Hat would look over at Texas Jack like it was all a big joke, then back at Billy Bob the same way. But I thought I could see a little something else in his face that he was trying not to give away. Surprise and pleasure.

Next thing Billy Bob told the crowd he was going to do was a thing I'd never seen him do before, and I felt certain that he was about to go from star attraction to jackass. It was a shot I'd heard him talk about, one Wild Bill used to make, but it was something he'd never tried, not even in practice.

He leaned over to Albert and said something, and Albert looked at him like he was crazy, then Billy Bob said, "Go on," loud enough that I could hear him, and Albert went back to the wagon.

"Ladies and gentlemen," Billy Bob said, "my father used to take a bottle with a cork in it, place it at thirty paces, and with a pistol shot, drive the cork into it and knock out the bottom of the bottle without breaking the neck. Never heard of no one else doing it, and I'd like to show you the spirits that guided my father now guide my hand."

Albert came back with the bottle, walked off thirty paces and set it up, then he legged it back behind the line Billy Bob had drawn in the dirt with the toe of his boot.

Billy Bob, without so much as blinking an eye, drew his pistol—the left one, mind you—and without so much as aiming, fired.

The shot drove the cork into the bottle and knocked out the bottom without breaking the neck.

The crowd cheered, and I'll tell you, so did I.

I reckon Texas Jack and Blue Hat didn't cheer, but they had their mouths open, and even when Jack got his cranked up, Blue Hat's stayed that way. Skinny dropped his bag of peppermints. It was a shot even an idiot could appreciate.

"Well, that's some damn good trick shooting," Texas Jack called out.

Billy Bob turned and looked in the direction of the voice. Texas Jack was elbowing his way through the crowd, and the crowd was stepping aside, fast.

"Thank you, fella," Billy Bob said when Jack was up close.

"Yeah," Jack said rubbing his chin, "that's about the best trick shooting I ever seen, except for Wild Bill himself."

"You seen Wild Bill shoot?"

"Yep, I did. Wasn't nobody could out-trick-shoot Wild Bill."

Billy Bob smiled. "Reckon not."

"But trick shooting isn't the same as facing a man with a loaded gun. That's a whole nuther thing."

The smile went off Billy Bob's face. "He proved he could do that too."

"With drunks and yellow bellies. He wasn't so big when John Wesley Hardin backed him down."

"That's just one of them stories," Billy Bob said.

"And when I backed him down."

"You?"

"Yeah. Name's Texas Jack."

For a long moment Billy Bob stared at Jack, looking for that Greek god he'd read about in them dime novels.

Jack stared back, opened his coat, and showed Billy Bob the butt of that fancy pistol. I don't think Billy Bob even noticed the pistol. He was still trying to fit that face with the one described in the books, and he wasn't having any luck at it.

Jack let his coat fall back over his gun, then turned and shouldered his way back through the crowd. When he reached Blue Hat he said, "Just like his pa," then the two of them snickered their way toward the saloon.

Billy Bob didn't even know he'd been called out, he was so amazed to see a dime-novel hero out walking around on two legs. But the truth of what happened slowly dawned on him. He turned to Albert and said, "Did that fella call me a coward?"

"No," Albert said quickly, "he was just funning."

"No, I think he called me a coward."

"He did that all right," one of the men in the crowd said, helpfullike.

Billy Bob turned to the man. "You think so?"

"Certain," the big-mouthed fella answered.

"It don't amount to nothing," Albert said, "just some old man shooting off wind. He most likely don't know Wild Bill from a pine knot."

"No," the big mouth said, "that there is the real Texas Jack, and he once backed down Wild Bill."

"The hell he did," Billy Bob said. "That's a lie. He didn't never back down no Wild Bill Hickok." He put his hands on his gun butts.

"Well," Big Mouth said, sort of fading back in the crowd a bit, "that's still Texas Jack."

Billy Bob looked at Albert, then he looked at me, then he looked at the crowd, which had started to shuffle.

Albert cleared his throat. "Ladies and gents, we going to bring on ole Rot Toe, the wrestling ape now. He's from the same place my folks come from, Africa."

"And he looks like your grandpa." It was Big Mouth again. Some of the crowd laughed.

Albert smiled like that was the kindest thing ever said about him. "Well now, that just might be for true, just might be. We colored boys ain't always sure who our folks are."

That got a big laugh. It sort of made me sick to see Albert do that, even if he was trying to turn the crowd's attention from Billy Bob and onto something new.

Albert led the crowd over to the ring, and Billy Bob, still standing like a cow that had gotten a lick from the butcher hammer, looked over to me and said, "Did that Texas Jack call me a coward? Was he making a showdown?"

"I didn't get it that way," I said.

"Yeah," he said, like he wasn't really asking my thoughts, just thinking out loud, "I reckon he did. Do you think that was the real honest-to-God Texas Jack?"

"He didn't look a thing like he was described in them dime novels, so I don't reckon it is."

"No. No he doesn't," Billy Bob said, and he walked back to the wagon kind of hangdog-looking.

I let out a sigh, figuring things were going to be all right, you know, and I went on over to the wrestling ring. When I got there, Albert had gotten Big Mouth to cough up some money and get in with Rot Toe.

Rot Toe was on a leash inside the pen, the leash was attached to one of the ring poles. He was also wearing a muzzle and gloves so he couldn't bite or tear an arm or leg off a fella. Big Mouth, who was pretty good-sized, had his shirt off and was holding his hands wide and waving them around like he was about to do some serious damage on that jungle ape.

"Now you give my grandpa a real hard time, hear me, Mister?" Albert said.

Big Mouth grinned at Albert through the netting. "I'm gonna choke him plumb to death."

"You do that," Albert said. "We can always make plenty more nigger grandpas, can't we?"

Big Mouth laughed. The crowd moved up close to the ring. Albert turned and saw me. He wasn't smiling like he had been. "Let Rot Toe go, Little Buster."

I went around to the other side and took the leash and collar off of him. "Go get him," I said.

And he did.

Big Mouth grinned when Rot Toe turned and started across for him, and I guess it was them red silk shorts we made Rot Toe wear for decency that made Big Mouth in a good humor. They were funny. But when Rot Toe dropped down to running on his knuckles, or rather them big, padded gloves, and Big Mouth seen the spit coming out between the muzzle straps, the color faded out of his eyes. It was too late for him to back down, and he'd already made a horse's ass out of himself in front of all them people, saying how he'd strangle Rot Toe and all.

Rot Toe grabbed Big Mouth by the head and leg, tossed him on the floor of the ring and jumped on him a bit. Big Mouth crawled off toward the netting, trying to find the place where Albert had parted it to let him in. But Rot Toe was used to that trick and he grabbed up Big Mouth again, this time by the feet, and slung him around in a circle, whipping him up in the air now and then like a bull whacker trying to crack a whip. Finally he let go and Big Mouth hit the netting and flopped back on the floor, his face and bare upper body marked with red net marks.

"You about to tire him," Albert chanted at Big Mouth. "Stay with it, he looks real weak."

Big Mouth screwed his face up, rolled to his feet, and yelled to Rot Toe. "Come get me, you ugly nigger."

Rot Toe grunted and waddled toward Big Mouth. Big Mouth ducked and rushed in on Rot Toe, grabbed him around the middle, tried to pick him up for a body slam. Rot Toe wasn't going for it though. He locked his gloved fingers into the edges of Big Mouth's pants and pulled them down with a jerk, which was another thing he did kind of regular which I forgot to mention.

Big Mouth's big, white butt was poking out at the crowd and ladies screamed at the sight of it, which seemed reasonable to me. I sort of felt like screaming. A few of the ladies, sticking to the fashion of the day, fainted, and there was one or two that just stared like maybe they was in shock. The men were laughing so hard it darn near drowned out Big Mouth's cussing and the sound of his feet as he beat a hasty circle around and around the ring.

You see, Rot Toe had run him the rest of the way out of his pants and was lazily following him on all fours, paying about half a mind to what was in front of him, and the rest of it to the crowd, which was cheering him on. Way Rot Toe bared his teeth looked a whole lot like a happy kid smiling.

Rot Toe finally got tired of the game, caught up with Big Mouth, snatched his feet out from under him and flung him up against the netting a few times, then dusted the floor with him six or seven strikes, and wandered off in a corner to pick at fleas on his chest.

Big Mouth inched his head around to sight Rot Toe, then started crawling for the spot where Albert had let him in. "Let me out," he was whispering, "let me out."

Albert was laughing so hard, looked as if he was going to go to his knees. Me and the crowd weren't doing bad neither.

Albert unhitched the place where the net lapped over, and Big Mouth, looking a lot less full of himself, crawled between it and flopped his naked butt to the ground.

A tall, gangly fella with a nose like a sun-dried cucumber smiled at Big Mouth and said, "Think you got him strangled yet, Harmon?"

Harmon didn't say a word. He stood up, and stiff as a soldier on parade, he walked off, his white rear end spotted with dirt, the sound of laughter rumbling like little, sharp thunders behind him.

• • •

When it turned dark, Albert hit the stage lanterns and got ready for Billy Bob to make his Cure-All talk. But two things happened right off to upset the apple cart. When I slipped behind the curtain to get Billy Bob to tell him it was time, he was gone. Wild Bill was still on the hand truck, and he was at the end of Billy Bob's stoop, his guns still cocked and pointing to where Billy Bob slept.

I went over to the head of the stoop and seen there was a dime novel lying there, parted, face down. I picked it up. It was *Texas Jack, Deadwood Pistol Demon, or The Shot That Never Missed*. It was one of the few dime books ever written entirely about Jack, though he come up mentioned in a few others.

I seen that the place it was open to was about the time Texas Jack was supposed to have backed down Wild Bill. The story said Jack opened his coat, showed his pistol, said "Name's Texas Jack," and stared at Hickok in a menacing manner, which I reckon was what he was doing to Billy Bob.

According to the book, Wild Bill said, "Jack, I have heard how fast and accurate you are with your revolver, and I confess that I want no quarrel with you," then Hickok turned and walked off, shaking a little.

Albert stuck his head through the curtain. "What's going on?" Then he seen there wasn't no Billy Bob.

"He's gone," I said. "After Texas Jack, I reckon."

"Damn." Albert stepped inside and rubbed his hand over his mouth. "We got a problem here, Little Buster.

"Well, Billy Bob does, as that's the real Texas Jack."

"Look, I can't go in no saloon, Little Buster, and I bet that's where he is."

Albert eyed me a moment. I sighed.

"You got to go talk him back to the wagon before there's some trouble."

"He don't listen to me."

Someone outside yelled, "There going to be a show or not?"

Albert stuck his head out from behind the blanket and said sweetly, "We just getting some things ready, any minute now."

When he pulled back inside he said, "It can't be helped, Little Buster. You got to talk him back."

"I don't even like him."

"I know."

"Oh, all right. I'll do my best."

"That's all I'm asking," Albert said. He picked up four juggling balls, a bottle of Cure-All from the rack, put his smile on, and went out to face the crowd.

I took off the derby I had on and put on my cap. I figured if I got killed I wanted to be wearing my cap and not no damn derby. I slipped out the back of the wagon, moved around to the edge of the stage.

Albert was juggling the balls and the bottle. "What we got in this here bottle," he was saying as he juggled, "is a miracle. That's right, folks, I ain't shy to say it, a miracle. You got piles? Don't answer that. They's womenfolk in the crowd. You got a belly bothers you when you eat spicy foods? Things just ain't right for you couple times a day, if you know what I mean? Your sight failing you some? We gots what you need right here, the little miracle, our Cure-All.

"Now, I know what you're saying to yourself. You're saying ain't no way I can afford a thing like this, a thing that is such a miracle, such a gift of medicine and the angels.

"Well now, it ain't free. I admit it. It does cost you something, but consider this. It fortifies the belly, makes the heart strong, and the list of folks that we have sold this Cure-All to and have come to us satisfied — no, not just satisfied, grateful, that's the word, plumb grateful to the point of crying — is endless. Never an unsatisfied customer.

"Now, I know what you're saying. Why don't he get on with telling us the price? Well, I'm coming to that, ladies and gents. I am. But I got to tell you that there ain't no medicine like this medicine. This will help you keep your youthful vigor and keep all your steps straight and your sight keen. It ain't even bad on taking out stains and using for a wash in your mouth to kill them smells you get from eating.

"And I tell you, ladies and gents, it ain't nothing but two bits a bottle. That's right. Two bits. I know it's hard to believe that something like this, a miracle in a bottle, comes this cheap. But it do. You see, we ain't here just to get your dollar, we're here to see you cured of your ills and made happy, and this here e-lixer is the thing to do it. Two bits, ladies and gents, two bits. Who's first?"

I looked at the crowd, seen he had their attention, went on around behind the wagon, and started up the street.

Thunder rumbled behind me. I turned to look. The sky back there looked dark even for nighttime.

Skinny had seen me, and he had left the crowd and was coming up the street toward me. I waited until he caught up. When he did, he turned and looked back toward the brewing storm, then back at me. He leaned forward, and with the peppermints on his breath overpowering his other smells, he said into my face, "Things is going to get bad."

I got a little chill. I thought of that other skinny fella that wasn't right in the head, and I thought of him grabbing Papa by the coat and saying abut how the wind was going to blow us away.

I didn't say anything to Skinny, I just nodded, went on over to the saloon, him following like a pet duck.

When we got to the boardwalk Skinny stopped and sat down, his back against the wall, his bag of peppermints between his legs.

I smiled at him.

He took a peppermint out of the sack and began sucking on it.

I took a deep breath and went inside.

• • •

Outside you could feel the storm coming, inside you could feel the same thing.

Billy Bob was over to the bar, leaning on it. Riley was putting a beer in front of him and looking around nervouslike.

At the back I seen that Blue Hat and Jack were at their same table. Blue Hat was looking at Billy Bob with a sort of slow burn. Texas Jack was trying to look bored and was sipping a glass of beer.

It was noisy in there, people chattering like squirrels, but it was an edgy kind of noise. I figured them chatterers could feel the tension between Jack and Billy Bob and were gleefully waiting for the first signs of bullets and bloodshed, not considering that a stray load could splatter what little smarts they had against the saloon wall.

While I was standing there, some of the crowd from our show drifted in, and after a quick look around, they joined the rest of the folks at the far left of the saloon and started to talk, never taking their peepers off Jack or Billy Bob.

To make matters worse, Billy Bob had his head turned toward Jack's table, and I'll bet you a chicken to an egg that Jack could feel those eyes on him as if they were two stones sitting on his head.

I made my feet move, went over to Billy Bob, and stood slightly behind him. "Billy Bob," I said softly, so he wouldn't think I was some fool sneaking up on him, "you need to come on back to the wagon. We're up to the Cure-All talk."

"You and the nigger do it," he said.

"But you're better at it," I said.

"I know that," Billy Bob said, "but I've come over here because I don't like being insulted, especially when it was a cowardly insult, kind you don't know's happening to you."

He said that part loud, and when he finished, the saloon went quiet as a church and all eyes turned to Texas Jack.

Jack looked over at Billy Bob, pursed his lips and said, "Is that a fact?"

"Since it come from a washed-up old geezer like yourself," Billy Bob said sweetly, "I couldn't take it for real at first."

"It was real," Jack said, and he stood up.

Blue Hat had gone cold on his stare, and when Jack stood, he got up and quietly faded away. Riley, over behind the bar, scratched the back of his neck casuallike and stepped briskly to the back, opened the door, and stepped out of sight.

"Billy Bob," I said, "forget it."

"Go back to your nigger," Billy Bob snapped, "and get out from behind me."

Sounded like good advice. I moved over to the left with the rest of the crowd.

"Maybe you ought to go back to the nigger too," Jack said, and he started easing around the tables toward Billy Bob. He got his foot hooked in a chair as he went, and tried to shake it off, and he got plumb crazy about it, started hopping around trying to get that chair rung off the top of his foot. We all held our hearts in our throats while he bounced about, because his face was getting red and puffy, and there ain't nothing like embarrassment to make a man come out shooting.

Eventually he got the chair shook off and made the end of the bar and stood there. He and Billy Bob were about fifteen or twenty paces apart. Jack had his left hand on the bar, his right was high at his side, pointing slightly inward toward the pistol at his middle. I seen that the hand on the bar was fluttering slightly, about as much as Billy Bob's legs were shaking.

"You handled that chair real well," Billy Bob said, and he let his lips pull up into a little smile.

"You should have been like your pa," Jack said, his voice cracking a little, "taken your insult and gone on. Live a lot longer that way."

"Ha!" Billy Bob said. "What's for me to back from. You didn't never back down Wild Bill Hickok, and you know it, and you won't back me neither."

"You sure?" Jack asked, almost politely.

Billy Bob nodded.

Somebody in the saloon chickened out. I heard him go through the bat wings, and when I turned to look they were swinging shut, and Skinny had walked over to take hold of them and look in. Maybe he didn't know exactly what was going on, but he knew it was exciting.

I looked back at Billy Bob and Jack. Silence was so heavy, had someone coughed about then, there'd have been shooting. I wanted to say something to Billy Bob, something that would make this whole thing stop, but nothing came to mind. And I sure as hell didn't want to draw attention to myself, lest he and Jack decide to start in on me first.

It was Jack that finally spoke, and he'd gotten the iron back in his voice. "Can I have your nigger when you're dead?"

"You can have that damn boy too," Billy Bob said. "But you got to get me dead first."

Jack took his hand off the bar and shrugged his shoulders. He said evenly, "You want to do this, kid?"

"You started it," Billy Bob said.

"What if you say you're sorry."

"Nope. You say you are."

"Nope. You know how many men I've killed, kid?"

"Ain't none of them me."

"That's the way you feel about it then?"

"Yep."

Jack stretched his neck, like his collar had gotten too tight. "Guess this is it, huh, boy?"

"Reckon so," Billy Bob said rolling his shoulders.

And Jack went for his gun.

He wasn't fast at all. I could have beaten him. Anyone could have. He was washed up, plain and simple.

But Billy Bob...well, try and picture this. One moment Billy Bob had his hands by his sides, the next they were full of pistols and the pistols fired and the left side of Jack's face jumped off in a spray of blood and bone and went all over the bar. Billy Bob cocked and fired both pistols again, and before Jack could so much as wobble, he caught two more bullets in his chest, and when they hit a spray of blood squirted out of his back and covered the wall behind him. I tell you, it was enough to make a billy goat lose his chow.

It couldn't have been long, but it seemed like Jack stood there for week, this surprised look on the side of his face that wasn't blowed off, and finally he folded up like a cheap pocketknife and flopped backwards to the floor, hitting his head so hard it sounded like thunder.

The saloon froze and the smoke from the pistols froze and no one breathed, until from the background someone said softly, "I'll be a sonofabitch," and that was what let the mortar loose. The world started to move again, the gun smoke twined upwards to the ceiling and Billy Bob put the pistols in his sash and let out a heavy sigh that was a cross somewhere between happiness and relief.

The chatter started again, louder and edgier than before, churning out fast and snappy like the loads from a Hotchkiss gun, and the crowd moved toward Billy Bob, and it was like little toads moving toward the king frog so he could croak loud and long for us, show us how it was done.

Riley, who had been peeping around the edge of the back door, came on out, tiptoeing and smiling. He leaned over the bar and looked at Jack, then he went around and bent over him.

"Dead," Riley said.

"You don't say?" Billy Bob said. "You mean splashing some beer on him won't bring him around."

Blue Hat came forward then, and things got quiet. We'd sort of forgotten him in all the excitement. He turned and looked at Billy Bob, then he walked over and looked at Jack. He bent down like Riley had done, and when he stood, he had Jack's pistol in his hand, which, by the way, Jack hadn't even managed to clear from his holster.

Blue Hat turned, holding the pistol loosely by the grip with a thumb and forefinger. He looked at Billy Bob. "I don't want no trouble," he said.

"That's good," Billy Bob said, but he sounded disappointed.

Blue Hat dropped the gun on the bar.

Riley, quick as a snake, sidled up to it, smiled at Billy Bob and said, "I'd like that as a souvenir."

"I was going to ask that," Blue Hat said to Billy Bob. "Jack said you was just a trick shooter, not a gunman."

Billy Bob glanced down at Jack's body. A messy, dark puddle was forming under it. "He ain't saying much of anything now, is he?"

"I ain't never seen shooting like that," Blue Hat said.

"And you won't again, unless it's me you see. You want that pistol, boy, take it. But unload it first. It would make me a mite more comfortable."

Blue Hat unloaded the pistol.

Riley watched him doing it, looking like a dog that had been kicked.

"You take them bullets," Billy Bob said to Riley.

"Yes sir," Riley said, just like it was the happiest thing he'd ever done. He scooped up the bullets, put them under the counter about where the Mexican's pistol was.

"And throw that ugly old liar out of here," Billy Bob said. "And mop up that blood, it's stinking up the place."

"Yes sir," Riley said. He ducked his hand behind the bar and got that same old rag he'd had the other day, went about mopping the counter off. The rag filled up quick, and I felt my stomach going. I tried to go for the door, but I couldn't make it. I put a hand on the bar and threw up on top of one of the stools.

When I lifted my eyes I seen Skinny looking at me over the bat wings. Next thing I knew Riley was putting a boot in my butt. "Get out," he screamed, "get out."

"Hold there," Billy Bob yelled. "Mind who you're kicking. He works for me."

I turned slightly and seen Billy Bob looking at me and Riley, and he was smiling. He looked ready to draw them pistols again. It didn't take much to know he was liking all this power. Wasn't no other reason he'd have stopped Riley from kicking me out. Any other time he'd have kicked me out his ownself.

"I'm sorry Mr...." Riley stuttered.

"Daniels," Billy Bob said. "Wild Bill Daniels. And you go on back to doing what you was doing. Get that trash out of here. Then clean up Buster's mess. He's been sick. Buster, come on over here."

I went. I didn't know what else to do. I hadn't managed to stop the fight, and I didn't know if I was glad Billy Bob was the one who won or not.

Billy Bob put his arm around me. "What'd you think of that, boy?" he said nodding at the spot where Jack still lay. Riley was getting hold of the body under the arms and was fixing to drag it out the back way.

I opened my mouth to say something, but nothing came out. Billy Bob didn't seem to notice. He slapped me on the back. "Barkeep. A whisky for my friend here. Whisky on the house."

That got a cheer from folks, and they started gathering around me and Billy Bob, and suddenly it was hot, real hot, and when I looked around me, it struck me how nobody looked like a person anymore. Their faces had changed. They had the same looks, you see, but there was something about the way they were smiling and the way their eyes looked that made me think that the souls had gone out of them.

Riley dropped Jack and started pouring glasses of whisky and beer, and suddenly I had a whisky in my hand, and I felt like I needed it, so I drank it, and the next thing I know I had another, and I drank it too.

"Ain't you got that stinker out of here yet?" Billy Bob yelled at Riley, and nodded at Jack's feet, which were now the only part of him you could see at the edge of the bar.

"But you said…" Riley started, then changed his mind. "Right," he said. He went back and got Jack and dragged him out the back door, and as he did, I got one last look at Texas Jack, Deadwood Pistol Demon, and he didn't look so special. He was just a fat, old, dead man with half his face blowed away. And there probably hadn't never been nothing special about him. He was just a sorry old loafer who lived off a storybook rep more than fact, and it had caught up with him. I figured that story Riley had told me about the Mexican was only half-truth. Jack most likely shot that sucker in the back and Riley's mouth took over from there.

Well, Riley got the mess cleaned up, and he came back and poured more drinks, and Billy Bob called for more, and I kept finding a whisky in my hand, and I kept drinking it. Each time I looked up from finishing one, the place had changed some. People looked odder and odder, even when I wasn't seeing them through the bottom of a whisky glass. Blue Hat was up by Billy Bob now, and it was like Texas Jack hadn't never been. The tick had dropped off the dead dog and was hooked onto another. The bony saloon girl was sitting on a stool next to Billy Bob and was entwined around him now, instead of the farmer, who had probably stayed home to do a bit of Bible study with his wife.

Riley was leaning over the bar and I couldn't get my eyes centered on nothing but his teeth, which seemed big and strong and ready to chew me or anything else up. His mouth was opening and closing, and it took a while before what he was saying to Billy Bob sunk into me. He was telling him about Homer, and saying what a bad hombre Homer was, and how he was even tougher than Jack, and he went on and on about the gunmen Homer had faced, and he told that

story he told me about him tracking down Wild Bill Longley
by himself.

I was dizzy, real dizzy. Too many Wild Bills. Wild Bill
Hickok, Will Bill Longley, Wild Bill Daniels.

"He ain't nothing but an old man," I blurted out.

"What's that?" Riley said.

"I said he ain't nothing but an old man. You said he was
an old man, seventy year old."

"Well now, boy, I ain't saying different now. I'm just telling Wild Bill here that Homer ain't gonna shine brightly on
finding out there's been a shooting in town."

I seen what Riley was doing, but couldn't put the thought
into words. I was too drunk. I had just come to that under-
standing. I'd never drank more than one whisky in my life,
and now here I was with a belly full of that hot, worthless
rot, and I was so drunk I couldn't make my mouth work. I
wanted to tell Riley to go to hell. I wanted to say to Billy Bob
that it was just Riley talking, trying to match him up with
the sheriff, trying to turn real life into a dime novel, but the
only thing that would come out when I finally got my mouth
open was what I said before. "Homer's an old man. You said
he was seventy year old."

"You said that already, hoss," Riley said, and I hated those
teeth of his. He didn't looked like nothing but teeth with a
set of eyes over the top of them.

"He's drunk," Blue Hat said.

Billy Bob laughed shortly, put his arm around my shoulders, and started walking me toward the door. I tried to push
against it, but I didn't have no iron in my legs. I think if Billy
Bob hadn't had his arms around my shoulders I'd have fallen
down.

"Seventy year old," I said. "He ain't no gunfighter. You
ain't neither."

Billy Bob pushed a little harder until we went through
the bat wings, then when we was out on the boardwalk out
of eyeshot of the drunks, he pulled me up close to him and

pressed his forehead against mine and whispered. "You're embarrassing me, you dumb fool."

"He ain't no gunfighter, just an old man," I said, but it sounded more like a mumble.

Billy Bob turned me around and kicked me in the butt. I went tumbling into the street.

"Go on back to the wagon and sober up, kid. Stay out of my sight tonight."

I didn't see Billy Bob go away. I wasn't seeing much of anything. I rolled over on my back and looked at the sky for a bit, then I closed my eyes. When I opened them everything was fuzzy, but someone was leaning over me, and he was thin and had his hands stuck out and there were guns in them, and for a moment I thought Wild Bill Hickok had gotten out of that box and come to pay me a visit.

"Bang! Bang!" It was Skinny's voice.

"Help me, Skinny. I'm sick."

Skinny leaned close enough that his face came out of the fuzz.

"Things is going to get bad." He stuck his fingers at me. "Bang!"

"I ain't for playing. I'm sick."

I closed my eyes again, and a moment later I felt hands on me. When I opened my eyes, Skinny was working with all his might to get me up. I gave it everything I had to help, but there just wasn't anything there.

Then Albert stepped out of the dark, pulled me to my feet, and slung me between him and Skinny. They hauled me away, the toes of my boots plowing trenches.

"I tried to stop him," I said to Albert. "I tried."

"I know, Little Buster."

"He killed Jack," I said. "That old man didn't have a chance. He wasn't nothing, Albert. I could have beat him. Anybody could."

"Hush up, Little Buster."

"I didn't know what to do, Albert. I tried but wasn't nobody listening to me."

"You did what you could. Wasn't no stopping them."

I got sick again. They stopped while I chucked up the whisky in my gut, but it didn't help me feel no better. They carried me to the wagon and laid me out on my old stoop.

"Not in here, Albert," I said. "Not here."

"Shush up, Little Buster. You just going to lay here while I fix you a bedroll outside. I'll come get you in just a shake."

"No, Albert," I said, but Albert was gone.

Everything was spinning. I turned my head toward Wild Bill and his box. It looked like that damned near skull face was grinning at me, and I swear to God there was a glint coming out of them bony sockets. The same glint I seen in Billy Bob's eyes after he'd killed Texas Jack. The glint he had when all them folks were gathered around him, trying to suck off the killing he'd done.

My eyes closed. I felt like I was whirling around and around. I could hear voices, though wasn't none of them American. It was them spirits in the wood. I knew it. They was talking to me. And though I couldn't make out a thing they were saying, I knew what it amounted to was the same thing Skinny had said: "Things is going to get real bad."

Chapter Six

I don't remember falling asleep, or when the voices went away — if there ever were any voices besides them inside my head — but when I woke up I was out of the wagon.

Albert had built a tent out of a tarp and had me under it. He and Skinny were inside with me. It was raining, I could hear it drumming on the tarp. I could hear the wind picking up too. It was still nighttime.

My mouth tasted dry and awful, like some rats had nested there. "The storm here?" I asked.

"Getting here," Albert said.

"We got to move on, with or without Billy Bob," I said. "He ain't going to go, Albert. He's gone a whole lot worse. I think he's got Wild Bill's gun spirit in him. You ain't never seen anything move as fast as he drawed on Jack. It was spooky, I tell you. With Wild Bill's shooting-iron spirit in him, and his own nasty disposition...Well, I think he's pushed too far, Albert, he'll kill most anybody."

"He won't kill me."

"He ain't the same, I'm trying to tell you."

"Bang," Skinny said loudly, drawing up both hands quicklike and pointing his fingers at me.

"Quit that now," Albert said. "Just quit it. It's making me shaky."

"He seen what Billy Bob done," I said. "He's mocking him." I propped up on one elbow. "I think we ought to go on without Billy Bob. Leave the wagon. Just get Rot Toe, sell some of our stuff and buy a couple mules, ride out of here."

"Can't," Albert said.

"You said yourself this was a bad town, Albert. You know that storm is coming and it ain't no regular storm. It's full of vengeance and it's Billy Bob it wants. But if we're here with that Hickok's body...We got to leave, Albert, you know that."

"I can't."

"What in Heaven's name has Billy Bob got hanging over you? It ain't slave days. You can do as you please. You don't owe him a thing. It don't make sense you letting him run your life like that."

"I got my reasons. Just shut up now, Little Buster. You're starting to make me mad."

I shut up. Skinny stretched out on the ground by me and fell fast asleep. I turned over and slept. Next thing I knew it was morning.

Skinny was still asleep, but Albert wasn't around. I got up and went outside. It was raining a steady drizzle and the sky was growling and lightning was flashing.

I went over to the wagon and found Albert inside looking at Wild Bill.

"He ain't nothing but bad luck," I said climbing inside. "Ain't nothing been good since we took him on."

"Wasn't all that good before we got him, was it?" Albert said, turning to look at me, "And before I picked you up, wasn't nothing for me to do but worry about Billy Bob. Now I got you too."

"Don't you worry none about me," I said. "I can take care of myself."

"You can, can you?"

"That's right. I'm seventeen now."

"So you are. Ain't nobody can take care of himself completely, Little Buster. We all needs someone sometime for something."

We were kind of smiling at each other then. I changed the subject before we got so chummy I felt like crying. "You ain't seen Billy Bob yet?"

"Stayed up last night waiting on him. He never showed."

"Still feel like you got to talk to him?"

"Yeah."

"When?"

"When he shows, I reckon."

He didn't show all that day. The storm got worse as time went on. The wind had gotten so high the trees were swaying on either side of the street and you could hear them groaning and you could hear the lumber in the buildings in town creaking.

We did some things to kill the time. We put Wild Bill in his box. We made sure Rot Toe was high and dry inside his tarp-covered cage. We fed and watered him. We took the mules over to the livery where they'd be more comfortable from the storm. We played some cards and cheated each other. Somewhere during the day Skinny came awake and wandered off, maybe going back to the saloon or bumming money for peppermints.

Finally it was dark, and still no Billy Bob.

We went out and took down the tent Albert had made, as the rain had run up under it and it wasn't a good place to lie anymore. We were folding it up, putting it in a corner of the wagon when Albert said, "I got no choice. I'm going over to the saloon. See if I can talk to Billy Bob."

"They'll kill you."

"If they don't, I reckon this storm will."

"All right, listen Albert. You got a mind to talk to Billy Bob, you let me go with you. I'll go in there and get him to come out. Try anyway. That way, no harm's done. Okay?"

"All right, Little Buster, we'll do it your way."

By the time we got to the saloon we were drenched from head to foot. The street was nothing but mud and water and the sound of the rain on the buildings was as loud as Indian drums. Or loud as I figured they'd be. I'd never heard any.

Skinny was standing outside the bat wings, his hands in his pockets, shaking a bit. The wind and the rain had brought some coolness with it. He smiled at us. We got up under the walkway porch with him and we all stood there for a while, shivering, looking out at the street.

"All right," I said finally, and I went inside.

Billy Bob was where I'd seen him last, and so was the bony saloon girl—wrapped around Billy Bob like a snake twisting on a limb. Riley was leaning over the bar, laughing at whatever Billy Bob wanted him to laugh at. Blue Hat was dangling on Billy Bob's every word, as if they were hooks.

I went over to Billy Bob. He didn't exactly look glad to see me, but he managed to be civil. "Buster. How you doing this fine day?"

"It's raining," I said.

"Not in here," he said, and everyone in the saloon laughed.

"It's the storm, you know?"

"Oh hell, don't start with the storm again," Billy Bob said, then he turned and told everyone about me and Albert believing the storm was haunted. That got him another good laugh.

When he was through, I said, "Albert's outside. He wants to talk to you."

"Anything a nigger's got to say can wait," Billy Bob said.

"This is important."

"I said it could wait, kid."

"Billy Bob!" It was Albert's voice, sharp and clear. Billy Bob shook that saloon girl off like a bulldog shaking off water. He stood, turned, and one hand came to rest on a pistol butt. Albert had his hands on top of the bat wings and he was looking at Billy Bob. He looked pretty stern.

"Don't you come in here," Riley bellowed.

"What do you mean calling to a white man like that, nigger?" Billy Bob said.

Albert let a strange smile work across his face. When he spoke it was the voice he'd used that day in Louisiana to keep Billy Bob from shooting that wife-beat fella. "I got to talk to you. Now."

"I don't want to hear nothing about no storm, dammit."

"It don't matter about the storm. We got to push on anyhow. We don't, you going to end up killing the sheriff."

"I ain't going to kill nobody unless they mess with me. Get on out of here and leave me alone, or I'm going to blow a hole in your black face. Hear?"

Albert held Billy Bob's gaze for a moment. "Have it your way, nephew," he said, and went away.

A look came over Billy Bob's face like I'd never seen before. It was sort of anger and sort of confusion. He went after Albert, and I followed on his heels, and the crowd followed out onto the boardwalk.

Billy Bob rushed out in the street, took hold of Albert's shoulder, and tried to spin him, but it was like trying to spin a tree. Billy Bob had to step around in front of Albert to stop him.

I was off the boardwalk now, out in the rain, easing toward them, Skinny tagging at my heels, and I was close enough to hear Billy Bob say, in an almost whining voice, "You're embarrassing me, Albert."

"I'm tired of this game," Albert said. "I could do worse."

Billy Bob shook, and I don't think it was from the cold. He stepped out of Albert's way and said loudly, "And remember that, nigger. Go on back to the wagon. I'll be there dreck'ly to give you a beating."

Albert wasn't paying him any mind. He'd started walking again.

Billy Bob straightened his shoulders and walked back to the saloon, pushing me with his shoulder as he passed. I heard him say something to the crowd on the boardwalk about uppity burr heads, then I was running after Albert, Skinny running after me.

I caught up with Albert and grabbed his arm. "What in hell was that nephew stuff about? He could have killed you. He's crazy, Albert. Can't you get it through your head. Crazy!"

"Don't start on me too. Take your hand off."

I let go and followed after him. "Albert, listen—"

"Don't never call me nephew again," I heard Billy Bob say.

Albert stopped walking.

I turned to look, fearing to see Billy Bob standing there with his hands hanging over his gun butts. But the street was empty. The crowd had gone back inside the saloon. There was just Skinny standing there pointing his fingers at us.

"Damn mockingbird," I said, snatching my cap off my head and slapping at Skinny with it. "You scared me half to death."

Skinny fell down on his knees in the mud, started crying, and covered his head with his hands against my cap beating.

"He didn't mean no harm," Albert said, grabbing my arm. "Leave him be." Albert took Skinny's elbow and helped him up.

"I'm sorry, Skinny," I said. "I didn't mean nothing." I put my cap on his head and patted him on the shoulder. He seemed comforted, like an old dog you say some easy words to after you've lost your temper and yelled at it.

Albert put his arms around both of us. "Come on, boys, let's go back to the wagon. Leave the town to those fools."

Chapter Seven

Ve hadn't been back at the wagon for more than an hour, I reckon, just in some dry clothes, when there came a hammering on the door and I took my hands from over the top of the lantern where I was warming them, and opened it.

It was Billy Bob. His hat had washed down over his face, and there in the glow of the lantern he looked like a crazy man. He smelled like a drunk. Which is what he was. He shot out a hand, grabbed me by the shirtfront, and tugged me out of the wagon into the mud and rain.

"And you nigger," Billy Bob yelled, "come out of there. And what's that idiot doing in here? Ain't them my clothes?"

"Only dry ones that would fit him," Albert said. "Mine are too big, Buster's too small."

I got up out of the mud, raked some of it off.

Billy Bob hadn't bothered to turn and look at me, and I'll tell you, the back of his head looked real inviting. I wanted to pick something up and brain him with it. But I didn't. I was scared.

"I don't care whose clothes are too big, and whose are too small," Billy Bob said. "You got no call to put my clothes on him."

Skinny was wearing one of Billy Bob's old, fringed outfits and some thick, wool socks. He was a hell of a sight. A sort of fool's version of Billy Bob, provided you could actually get more foolish than Billy Bob.

"Come out," Billy Bob raved. "And bring that simple head with you. I'm going to give him a thrashing."

Skinny's eyes darted ever which way. He was used to being in trouble for things he didn't understand, and he was used to looking for a way out. With the wagon wall back up in place there wasn't but one way to go, and that was out that door, right into Billy Bob's arms.

"Tell you what," Albert said easing toward the door. "You give me that thrashing, nephew."

"Don't call me that," Billy Bob said.

"That's what you come here for, ain't it? Ain't that what you told them? That you was going to come back here and give your nigger a thrashing?"

Albert stepped out into the rain, closed the door behind him.

Billy Bob stepped back. He said something, but I didn't catch it because thunder rumbled real loud. Whatever it was, you can bet it was a mouthful of sin.

"Thrash me," Albert said, and he took a step forward. "Get your nigger in line. Thrash me."

Billy Bob stepped back. "You forgot whose wagon this is?" Billy Bob said.

"I ain't never forgot whose wagon this is," Albert said.

"You got no call to come over to the saloon like that, talk that way in front of my friends."

"Friends? You call that mess friends? You just a circus passing through to them, nephew."

"Don't call me that no more, don't never call me that no more, never, never, hear? It ain't right for a nigger to...Don't do it, you hear?"

Albert stepped right up to him. "I hear, *nephew.*"

Billy Bob went for his pistols, and even drunk he was fast. But it didn't do him no good. When Albert had stepped close, he put his hands just above Billy Bob's pistol butts, and Billy Bob's hands pushed Albert's down on the guns.

Albert drew the pistols out of Billy Bob's sash, stepped back and held them loosely. "Darky trick," he said.

Albert put one of the pistols under his arm and began unloading the other, letting the shells drop in the mud.

"Now don't do that, Albert," Billy Bob said. "That ain't right."

Albert began unloading the other pistol. He stepped over to Rot Toe's cage, threw back the tarp, and tossed both pistols between the bars. Rot Toe waddled over, picked one of them up, and smelled of it.

"You...you tell your grandpa to hand those out," Billy Bob said.

Albert stepped toward Billy Bob quickly, and Billy Bob swung.

Albert didn't even try to block or duck. Billy Bob's fist caught him on the side of the head, but Albert's head barely moved. Albert grabbed Billy Bob by the shirt collar with one huge hand, used the other to slap Billy Bob. He did that three or four times, real quick, then he shoved Billy Bob into the mud.

Before Billy Bob could scramble up, Albert had him by the back of the collar and the seat of the pants, and he lifted and drove Billy Bob's head into the mud a few times, sucking the hat off his head, filling his mouth and eyes with muck.

Rot Toe was hopping up and down in his cage, chattering wildly, banging one of the pistols against the bar. He was like a drunk at a girlie show.

Now Albert had Billy Bob upright again, and had gone back to slapping. Every time he'd slap, mud would fly out of

Billy Bob's hair and his knees would droop. When Albert got tired, he just let Billy Bob fall back on his butt in the mud. About that time, Skinny opened the door of the Magic Wagon and looked out. He saw Billy Bob sitting in the mud, the rain washing streams of the same out of his hair and down onto his face. Skinny let out with a strange laugh. It sounded a lot like a cow bawling. He jerked both fingers at Billy Bob, said, "Bang."

Shivering more from anger than the cold rain, Billy Bob stood up. He looked first at Albert, then Skinny, then me, and when he did I felt weak. There was pure murder in his eyes.

He picked up his muddy hat and shook the mud off of it and put it on. He pointed a finger at Albert. When he spoke he sounded almost winded, but it was just plain mad, is what it was. "You make that monkey hand over my pistols now. You hear?"

"You make him," Albert said.

Billy Bob took a deep breath, cut Albert to pieces with a look, and went over to the cage. "You give me those," he said to Rot Toe, and he shot a hand out and grabbed at the one Rot Toe was holding.

Rot Toe grabbed Billy Bob's wrist, jerked him forward until Billy Bob slammed against the bars. Using the pistol in his other hand, Rot Toe reached through the bars and slammed the butt against Billy Bob's noggin. It was such a hard lick it creased Billy Bob's hat to his skull and sent him dropping to his knees. Had Rot Toe not been holding him by the wrist he'd have fallen over. Rot Toe reached through the bars and whacked Billy Bob a couple more times with the pistol, and was just really starting to enjoy himself when Albert said, "Let him go, old man."

Rot Toe looked at Albert. For a moment, I didn't think he was going to do it, but he let go. He waddled back to the center of the cage and sat down, huffed up like a kid that's had a toy taken from him.

Albert went over and pulled the tarp down on the cage. He pulled Billy Bob up and pushed him back against it. He slapped Billy Bob on the face lightly a few times. One of Billy Bob's eyes opened, then the other. Albert let go and stepped back. Billy Bob managed not to fall down. He shook his head, took some long breaths, and staggered away from the cage toward the street. "You'll pay. All of you," he said. "You can't do this to the son of Wild Bill Hickok."

He stepped into the street and squished across the mud and over into the woods. We heard him crashing around out there for a while, then Albert said, "Let's go inside," and we did.

If my suit wasn't ruined, it was darn close. Except for Skinny, who was still high and dry, we were soaked to the bone. Albert and I took off our clothes and strung them on a line across the wagon, then we wrapped ourselves in blankets and sat on the stoop. I didn't feel so good. I had a slight fever and sniffles.

When we were as warm as we could get, Albert said, "Little Buster, I think it's time I told you some things so you'll understand. I'd like you to just sit quiet until I'm finished."

• • •

"When I was a boy, Little Buster, I was the son of an ex-slave during the worse time you can imagine, next to slave days themselves. It was called Reconstruction, and I know you've heard of it. We coloreds was supposed to be freemen that could work for our living, just like whites, but wasn't too many folks would hire us, not for any kind of work. Most of them had gotten used to getting it from us for free, and wasn't in the mood to start paying for it. Part of it was the Yankee government. They was telling folks they was supposed to hire us cause the Yankee president said so, and people didn't cotton to that much.

"Lot of whites blamed us coloreds for their misery, cause of the way the Yankees was pushing on them. And to tell it true, Little Buster, them Yankees hurt us all in the long run cause they turned their winning into such a mean thing.

"Well now, I heard tell that the Army was hiring coloreds, and I heard too that they paid and you got to wear a pretty uniform. I heard they treated you near good as whites, and that some coloreds had even made sergeant, which was as far as they'd let a dark man go. Sounded like the life to me. I went out West and joined the Cavalry, was out there for years.

"I'll tell you, Little Buster, the Army wasn't no paradise, fighting Indians and all. And we coloreds fought more Indians than damn near anybody, but you don't hear tell of that. Or if you do, you just hear it was the Army done it, and they don't mention it was a colored troop what was the ones doing all the shindigging.

"Still, being a man in the Army was a whole sight better than being a nigger out of it, and sometimes I figure I should have stayed there. But I didn't. I quit and joined up with a fellow named Doc Madonna, and Madonna was a fine man. Didn't see no colors at all. He just saw a man. He made me a partner after a time, and we traveled the country selling medicine, not claiming it could do more than it could do, and we did some juggling and such. Wasn't bad at all.

"But Doc died and the wagon was left to me. For a while I done what we'd been doing, but it just wasn't the same without him. I got tired of it and went back to East Texas, looked up my family.

"When I got there I found that my daddy had died some time back, and wasn't long after my mama had taken up with a white man on account of she needed the money he paid her, and this white man gave her a child, and that child was thirteen when I come home. Her name was Jasmine. She was what you call a high yeller. Pretty thing.

"Well, I figure Mama done the best she could and all, having all them mouths to feed, so I didn't judge her none. And besides, that white man was long gone and all the kids except Jasmine had grown enough to go off on their own, get a little farm work and such, start their own poor families.

"I got me some work fixing things here and there, working some in the blacksmith shop. Little farm work from time to time. Anything to turn a dollar.

"Well now, to make a long story short, Little Buster, Mama died three years later, and Jasmine, she got in with this white boy and she got with child. That white boy got tired of her real quicklike, and he didn't come around no more. She didn't never tell me who he was, and it was a good thing, or maybe I'd have had to turn his head around on his shoulders some, and that wouldn't have done me or nobody no good.

"This baby was born, and him being the son of a white man and a high yeller, he come out looking white as you. Only thing he had that was like the family was the little red star birthmark low on his back. Jasmine had it. I have it, though you can't see it as good on me cause of me being a colored. But on her and on this boy it showed up good.

"Now there didn't seem a thing for her to do but to put this child on a white's doorstep. For Jasmine to have a white baby would have meant she and that child would have been treated worse than slaves, but she figured she could pass him for white and get him in with a good family and all, and he'd grow up having a chance. She picked this family, the Daniels, cause they had money and seemed like pretty good folks. She left the baby on the doorstep, and sure enough they took him in and they raised him white, as they didn't know that he wasn't.

"This boy they named Billy Bob and he grew up not wanting a thing. He had coloreds at his feet cleaning the floors, dusting the house, and he never knowed he was one of them.

"Jasmine got her a job working for the Daniels as a maid, and that way she got so she could keep an eye on him. And it didn't make her happy. He treated her and all the coloreds like dirt, cause the Daniels may have been good in their way, but they figured a nigger was just some kind of animal that you could teach to clean the furniture, and wasn't good for much else, and Billy Bob, he was just like them.

"There was this buggy accident, and the Daniels, the ones that had become Billy Bob's mama and daddy, was killed in it, and when that happened, the children started scrambling to get the inheritance. Billy Bob being just a took in child, and there not being no will, didn't end up with nothing but his name. They put him out of the house and on his own.

"Jasmine should have just let it end there, let him go on and live as a white man, but I figure it was eating her inside, being his mama but not getting to tell him. And maybe she thought if he knowed he'd come from black folks well as white, he'd straighten some, not be so hateful toward coloreds, grow up to be a better man.

"Well, she told him. Proved it with that red star on her back, and he went darn near crazy, knocked her down and run off. Jasmine come and got me and I went to get him, had about half a mind to beat him to death, but I found him drunk in a ditch and took him home to Jasmine.

"He wasn't no count even sober, and took to cussing his mama, saying it wasn't so, that he wasn't no nigger, and I don't have to tell you how bad it distressed her, Little Buster. But he was still her boy and she loved him. I reckon I felt for him too. He was my nephew and he didn't ask to be part white and part colored, but I couldn't help but think that boy just had him a bad streak, and knowing what he knew now was just making it wider.

"He didn't go into town no more, he was so ashamed, though there wasn't nobody knowed the truth but him and us. Still, it gnawed at him. He'd eat at the house, cut a little firewood, but most of the time he just stayed wandered off in the woods.

"Wasn't long before Jasmine took the chest cold bad, and I think some of the reason she was so sick was worry over that boy. Well, she up and died. But before she did, she made me promise I'd take care of that boy, see to it that he got some kind of trade and such. He could already read, write, and cipher, so she thought if I could just get him on the right road, he'd grow up and be a good boy. Mama talk, you know?

"I buried her the same day I made the promise, cause she didn't last long after I'd give her my word, and Billy Bob, he didn't even come watch the burying. He couldn't get out of his head that she was the same woman who'd cleaned his messes in the Daniels house, and a part of him—the biggest part—seen her as nothing more than a nigger.

"Like I said, he was my nephew and I made a promise to Jasmine, and I guess I figured there had to be some good in him, being partly of her blood, so I took to caring for him.

"That old wagon I'd gotten from Doc Madonna was parked out back of my shack, which was a thing I'd throwed up next to Jasmine's place, and it come to me I could teach Billy Bob the medicine show business, as it was the only thing I really knowed about. Sort of let him run the show, you see. Him looking full white could make it a whole sight easier than me doing it by myself and being a colored.

"That must have been where I messed up. Or maybe it just added to things. But him becoming boss and playing like he was full white just made him more that way in his head. Wasn't long before I'd have to come down on him hard when he got to playing it all too well.

"Still, it wasn't bad for a time. Then he took to reading them dime novels, thinking about them gunfighters and how they was all so handsome-looking and brave—and white—and he was just looking for some reason not to accept being of colored blood, so he'd go off in these dream worlds, and wasn't long before he was pretty much believing them.

"He took up the gun too. Started learning to trick shoot. And it was like he was born to it. The better he got with that gun, worse things between us got. Then you came along and the secret had to be hidden all the harder. Then we got that body in the box, and that stuff he'd been saying about being the son of Wild Bill Hickok really went to his head. Well, you know that part. And there's that curse, and this town…and I'll tell you, Little Buster, I haven't done so good by the promise I made Jasmine. So you can see why I can't just go off and leave him. He's family. He's blood."

• • •

I sat there when Albert was finished, kind of dazed. Like someone had bent a fire iron over my turnip.

"But… what can you do, Albert? You've done all there is to do. He ain't worth it."

"I still got to try, Little Buster. You see now why I got to. A deathbed promise is a sacred thing."

We didn't say much else. Just found places to lie down. And though I wasn't in the mood for sleep, I was tuckered, and that fever of mine had gotten worse.

The fever sent me down in a deep well of sleep, and down there were the waters of a dream. It was the one I'd had before, the one about Mama in the house, flying away to Oz, her red hair flapping like flames. I hadn't had it in some time. The fever I guess. That and the storm blowing, building outside the wagon until it shook and the roof rattled with rain like a dozen men with hammers beating it with all their might, fast as they could go.

So I was deep into this dream when there came a sound that wasn't part of it. Not thunder or lightning. Just a sharp crack, and it took me a long, deep moment before I realized it was a gunshot.

I got up. I was dizzy and as hot as if I had been bedded in coals. I turned the lantern up, seen that Albert was gone, and Skinny was stirring.

Pulling on my wet pants, I went outside. Albert, wearing nothing but a blanket, was standing by Rot Toe's cage. The tarp was off the cage and the door was open. It looked to have been pried with a bar. Rot Toe was gone and so were the pistols. When I got over close, I seen there was a puddle of blood on the bottom of the cage, mixing with the wooden floor and the rain.

"Billy Bob?" I asked.

"Had to be," Albert said. "I should never have left them pistols in there. Should have known Billy Bob would come for them. Come on, Little Buster, Rot Toe's hurt. We got to find him."

We got dressed in our wet clothes, and Skinny came with us. We looked high and low for sign, but the rain had washed most of it away. We did find a few cracked limbs across the way, a tuft of Rot Toe's hair on a limb, but when we got in the woods and started looking, we didn't see another sign of him.

Those woods were giving me the shakes, and I don't mind telling you. It was like this whole little section of the world, the woods, this damned town, had been given over to the devil as some kind of playground.

Finally we had to give it up, go on back to the wagon. When we got there, we found the back door open and flapping in the wind. And Wild Bill Hickok and his box were gone.

"We was suckered," Albert said. "Suckered to the bone."

About that time, our thoughts were taken from what had happened by cussing. This wasn't your plain old cussing, this was the stuff of a real professional. A fella that had had some practice at it and knew it wasn't just a matter of words but a way of life.

It had just gone light, so we got a good look at what was coming, and it was a sight. Down that muddy street there came a team of six mules. They were pulling a long, flat sled, which looked to have been thrown together in a hurry, and standing at the front of it was a tall, skinny fella with a washed-down hat and a face so thickly overgrown with hair it looked like a badger's butt. He was cussing now and then to keep rhythm, but the real cussing, the good stuff, was coming from another man.

There was a horseless carriage on the sled, and sitting on the seat, the rain beating down on him, was an old fella with white hair sticking out from under his hat, and a white mustache that darn near covered his whole mouth. He had his arms crossed, was looking straight ahead, and he was cussing every breath, letting it roll out like a poem. Though, unlike a poem, it wasn't embarrassing and didn't make you want to look the other way.

The horseless carriage's wheels and underbottom were all caked with mud, and I figured it had gotten stuck bad and he'd had to get this fella with the mules and the sled to haul him out, and he wasn't happy about it.

Far as I was concerned, he got what was coming to him there. Those newfangled noisemakers weren't never going to catch on. They couldn't travel the country the way a horse could, and you couldn't grow feed for them. They were ugly too.

They cussed on down the street, and we watched after them. When they got past the saloon, I lost interest and turned away. But Albert didn't.

"Uh oh," he said.

I turned to look again. A crowd was coming out of the saloon. Billy Bob was in the lead. They were walking toward the sled. The sled had stopped and the man sitting in the horseless carriage got down and stepped into the street. He turned toward the crowd, to figure what was going on, and when he did, the sun winked off of his badge and I knew who he was.

We started running.

When we got close I heard Billy Bob yell, "You won't take me alive, sheriff."

And the sheriff said, "What's that?"

"Draw if you got the guts," Billy Bob said.

"What's that?" the sheriff said again.

And Billy Bob pulled both of his revolvers and shot him.

When he did, the fella who owned the mules, thinking that it might be open season, jumped off the sled on the other side and went facedown in the mud.

The sheriff took a careful step forward, and sat down, his butt coming to rest on the edge of the sled.

Billy Bob turned and watched Albert and me come up. He smiled.

I went over to the sheriff, bent down beside him. His face was as white as a china plate. He looked at me.

"I'm sorry," I said. "We wanted to stop him."

"What's that?" he said.

"I'm sorry."

"Can't hear so good," the sheriff said. He looked back at Billy Bob, who was still smiling, pushing his pistols into their sash.

"Who in tarnation was that?" the sheriff said. "And what in hell have I done to him?"

"It don't take a thing," I said.

The sheriff's head rolled, his hat fell off, and he sagged against me. I put his hat back on, pulled him onto the sled. When I had him laid out, I seen that he'd been hit twice in the chest, about a hand's span apart. It looked as if his shirt were decorated with two big, wet buttons, and they were still growing.

I turned to Billy Bob. "He didn't hear a word you said. He was darn near deaf."

"That ain't so," Riley offered, helpfullike, pushing up to the front of the crowd. "Homer, he had a built-in *instink* for them things. He knew Billy Bob was going to draw, he just wasn't fast enough to match him."

"He didn't even know what it was all about," I said.

"Just saved me having to explain about Jack before I shot him," Billy Bob said, and he got his laugh from the crowd. And some crowd it was. Those folks were right flexible. If Homer had drawn on and beat Billy Bob, they'd have been standing next to him, patting him on the back, telling him what a great sheriff and gunfighter he was. They were nothing more than a kind of vulture, feeding themselves off the pride of whoever was riding high at the time.

Billy Bob's head floated to his left and his eyes narrowed. When I looked, I seen he was staring at Skinny. I'd forgotten about him. He'd followed along behind Albert and me like a puppy, anxious to see what was going on. Way he was smil-

ing, you figured he thought this whole mess had been put
together for his amusement.

"Hey, dummy," Billy Bob said, "you're still wearing my
duds."

Skinny smiled big and nodded.

"I don't like that none," Billy Bob said.

Blue Hat, who'd been standing next to Billy Bob, said,
"Make him take them off."

Billy Bob smiled. "That's an idea. Take off them clothes,
idiot."

Skinny looked confused. He looked to me, then to Albert.

"Leave him alone," Albert said to Billy Bob.

"You ain't got no say-so at all in this matter, nigger," Billy
Bob said.

Albert walked slowly over to Billy Bob. "I said, leave him
alone."

Maybe Billy Bob would have shot Albert, I don't know.
What happened was Blue Hat, who was standing a little to
the side, jerked Jack's old pistol, and hit Albert a lick upside
the head.

Albert wheeled, grabbed Blue Hat, and jerked him into
the muddy street. Before Blue Hat hit the mud, Billy Bob
had drawn his pistols, and, whipping the barrels from left to
right, he hit Albert about six times. He was real quick.

Still, Albert didn't go down right then. It was when the
crowd joined in, hitting and kicking, that he went down.

I tried to get over there, but as I went I ran past where
Blue Hat was getting up, and about the same time I stepped
on his hat, he grabbed my ankle and pulled it out from under me. I went down in the mud and my head hit the edge of
the boardwalk and I went on a short, dark trip.

When I came out of it, I could hear Billy Bob saying to
Skinny, "Take off them clothes, idiot, or I'm going to start
shooting them off of you."

I raised up some, looked to my left and seen Albert lying
in the mud. Blue Hat had gotten up now, had his hat in one

hand, and was kicking Albert in the head as hard as he could and as many times as he could.

I tried to say, "Stop it," but a hunk of mud fell out of my mouth, and by then he'd quit kicking.

I heard a pistol shot, and I rolled on my side and seen Skinny standing there, startled, holding his hand out to his side. He turned slowly and looked at it. His left little finger was gone. Billy Bob had shot it off.

"Take off the clothes, dummy," Billy Bob said. "Or the next one's in your head."

"Go ahead and shoot him," I heard Blue Hat say. "He ain't good for nothing. Ain't got nobody but this nigger and that fool."

"Take the clothes off," I croaked at Skinny.

Blue Hat kicked me in the back of the head and I rolled forward some, got to a knee and said it again, "Take them off, for Heaven's sake, Skinny, take them off."

Blue Hat must have come up behind me and clubbed me with his pistol then. I don't know, but I went down in the mud again.

"Take off the clothes, dummy. Take off the clothes, dummy. Take off the clothes, dummy," echoed again and again, and when I looked up, I knew why. It was Skinny mocking Billy Bob perfect.

"You stop that," Billy Bob said.

But Skinny was smiling again. He was still holding his hand out to his side, and it was dripping blood, but he wasn't paying it any mind. He had a new game to play. "Take off the clothes, dummy," he said, and started to wave his right hand around like he had a pistol in it.

"You hear me?" Billy Bob yelled. "You stop that."

"You hear me?" Skinny said. "You stop that."

"Damn you," Billy Bob said, and he shot Skinny right through the heart.

I don't remember seeing Skinny fall. I must have passed out again about then. It was the fever, the beating, and the gol-darned sorriness of it all did me in, I reckon.

Next thing I knew my head was floating up from the mud and there was light in my eye.

When the light got so it wasn't hurting, and everything around me quit spinning, a voice said, "You dead, boy?"

It was the fella that had been driving the sled, and my head wasn't floating. He was holding my head out of the mud by the hair.

"I'm peachy," I said.

"You don't look peachy." He got his arms under mine and got me to my feet. When I was standing, I wobbled over to Albert, fell down on my knees beside him. "Albert," I said. "Albert, you with us."

His hand fluttered and I took hold of it. "God, Albert. Say you're okay."

"Most of them licks he got was in the head," Sled Driver said. "Nigger has a hard head. That idiot fella's dead as a rock."

"Albert," I said again.

"Here…Little Buster. Here."

"Help me," I said, looking up at the fella.

Sled Driver got an arm, I got the other, and we pulled Albert over to the boardwalk and propped his back against the general store wall.

"I'm going to be okay," Albert said. "Things has quit spinning around. I don't think I'm busted inside."

"Cause you got most of it in the head," Sled Driver said kindly. "You people can take a lick to the head."

Albert turned his swollen face slowly upwards, looked at the man with the badger's butt for a face. I thought maybe he was going to try and get up and smash the man's head, but he didn't. He said, "You take a message to the saloon for me?"

"Hell no," the sled driver said. "That crazy fella and his circus is over to the saloon."

"We'll pay you," Albert said.

"What message?" I said.

"How much?" Sled Driver said.

Albert pushed a hand in his pants and fumbled out six bits.

Sled Driver looked at the six bits in Albert's palm. "No way. Not chancing getting myself made into a lead sandwich for no six bits."

Albert turned his head to me.

"I got some," I said. I dug out all I had. Together it was about four dollars.

"That enough?" Albert asked.

"Well now," Sled Driver said. "Four dollars is four dollars."

"Just asking you to take a little message. You let me and Buster here get back down to that wagon at the end of the street, then you tell him this. His uncle, Private Albert C. Moses, United States Cavalry, is coming to see him. And I ain't bringing presents. Tell him I ain't coming for no fast draw. I'm coming to do a bit of business."

"That don't make no sense," Sled Driver said.

"It will to him," Albert said. "Little Buster. Get me on my feet."

I did.

"Is he going to shoot me?" Sled Driver asked.

"Not if you tell him that dumb, crazy nigger he beat up sent the message. Then you can cuss me some. He likes that."

"Well," Sled Driver said looking at the money in his hand, "four dollars is four dollars."

• • •

We carried Skinny back to the wagon and put him on Billy Bob's stoop. Albert pulled the rack of Cure-All aside, and underneath it was a trap door.

"Madonna and I built this in here," Albert said. "Billy Bob didn't never know about it."

He opened the trap. Inside was a crate. He took the crate out and opened it. There was an old Army uniform, a cap, a

.45, an old .44, and a Springfield rifle, some shells for all of them.

"Now," Albert said, "I got this thing to do. You ain't no part of it. You go over to the livery, get the mules, hitch them up, and get out of here."

"What about you and Rot Toe?"

"I'll come on to the next town later. Hang around a day or so here and see if I can find Rot Toe. I don't come, you just keep on without me."

"I can't do that."

"You're a good boy, Little Buster, but you don't know a thing about fighting men. I used to make a living at it."

"You can't go after him alone. He'll have Blue Hat with him. Maybe someone else. This ain't no dime novel, Albert."

"I don't plan to have no straight draw with him, Little Buster. I'm just going to kill him. I owe that much to Jasmine. I said I'd watch after her boy, and I done all I could. This is the last thing I got to do for her. Get him out of the way. He can't carry on her blood and be the way he is. Ain't right."

"Can't let you go alone, Albert."

"You got no choice. You look plumb sick anyway, Little Buster. You ain't up to it."

"I'm up to it. I'll just follow you if you don't let me go."

Albert sighed. "All right," he said.

He put on the soldier suit. It was a little tight, but still fit him. He stuck the .44 in his belt, put the extra shells for it and the Springfield in a pocket. He gave me the .45. "That kicks," he said. "Use two hands. And remember. You're just the backup, so stay out of it best you can."

I nodded.

We went out of there down the street, and the woods, the buildings, even the sky, seemed to be pushing down on me. It was the fever made it seem that way, I guess. Even the .45 in my hand seemed unreal. The barrel two yards long, the hammer as big as a cucumber. I kept blinking until I brought things into focus, but it didn't stop the throbbing and rushing in my head.

The storm had turned something fierce, and my cap brim had gone soggy and was slapping in my face like the flap on a union suit.

When we got to the saloon, Albert sent me around back. I hoped the door wasn't locked. I wondered if Albert had sent me back there just to get me out of the way.

Jack was still out back. They hadn't gotten around to burying him yet. Even in the wind and rain he had him an aroma. He was all swollen up too. So big, in fact, his shirt had rolled up under his arms and his pale belly looked like a polished, white boulder. Ants and such had been at him. Maybe a stray dog.

I stepped over Jack, put a hand to the door and eased it open. There wasn't a sound in there. No one took a shot at me.

I pushed it open some more and stepped inside, and then I seen why it was so quiet.

Albert had already come in, big as a brass band, the rifle over his left shoulder, the .44 in his right hand.

Everyone was just staring, not quite believing it.

"Nice day, ain't it?" Albert said.

"You got a lot of sand, nigger," Riley said, easing to the middle of the bar.

I stepped in where everyone could see me and said, "You stay away from under there, Mr. Riley," I said. "That Mex's pistol will just get you killed. In fact, you just take it by the barrel and put it up easy on the bar, slide it down to the far end out of the way."

He did.

Albert had the rifle level now, waving it toward Riley and the pistol toward the crowd at the tables. They were all looking very friendly, and every hand was in plain sight, lest there be a mistake.

"Where's Billy Bob?" Albert said.

"Gone to church," Riley said. "He didn't trust no nigger to come here and fight fair. He said to meet him there."

"Anybody with him?"

"Just the kid, Noel. Billy Bob figured you'd bring your boy here. He wanted to even things up."

"Guess that means you had to give Noel back them bullets, huh?" I said.

Riley didn't look at me.

Albert grinned at Riley. "We'll have a whisky, Riley. Set us up a bottle."

"I don't serve niggers. Ain't never. Ain't going to."

Albert whipped the Springfield around and fired. The shot hit the sign that said: WE DON'T SERVE NIGGERS, FREED OR OTHERWISE, and knocked it off the wall.

The crowd found places under tables and Riley turned several shades of white, including one that matched Texas Jack's belly.

Riley swallowed, turned, got a bottle and two glasses, put them on the bar, and stepped back.

"No, you pour, Riley," Albert said. "In fact, get you a glass and have one with us."

Riley's face did all manner of tricks, but he got another glass and put it on the bar. Albert went over to the bar and motioned to me. Riley poured us all a drink.

I needed that shot of whisky like I needed a railroad spike in the head, but I drank it. Albert lifted his with Riley, making sure it went down about the same time as the barkeep's.

"Now wasn't that good?" Albert said. "Me and my old friend, Riley, taking a drink together. We'll do it again, won't we?"

Riley's lip jumped a little.

"Well, it's been fun, but we got to go shoot us some boys," Albert said. He went down the bar, got the Mex's gun, put it in his belt.

We backed out of the bar and through the bat wings, stood out on the boardwalk looking at the storm and the street. Across the way I could see Sled Driver. He'd given the message and got out of there. He was leaning against a building looking at us. I reckon he wanted to see how it all came out, and still be a distance from it. When he seen I was looking at him, he gave me a little wave from the hip, like maybe I ought to be glad to see him.

Why not? He did help me out of the mud. I waved back.

"Well," said Albert, "it's going to take the edge off things if we have to go back in there and ask where the church is."

"I know where it is," I said.

• • •

We didn't talk as we walked down the boardwalk. In fact, it was about all I could do to stand. I felt like someone was building a brush fire inside me.

Across the way, pacing us step for step, was Sled Driver. Once I looked back and seen that the crowd from the saloon was following us.

Albert pulled the Mexican's pistol out of his belt and shot at the boardwalk in front of them a few times, and they disappeared down it, and into the saloon like rabbits being chased by a hound.

"They just like to watch," Albert said. "They ain't so much for getting shot at."

"Me neither," I said.

We passed the sled with the horseless carriage on it. The mules had been taken away, but the sheriff was still there, though someone had gone to the effort to set him in the seat of his rig. His head was slumped, and he just looked like he was resting in the rain.

By the time we come to the end of the boardwalk and the overhang, there wasn't nothing but rain and wind and darkness, and that big yellow lightning cutting now and then, and once when it flashed bright we saw the church.

We were almost on top of it. It was small with a cross on the steeple, shutter doors at the top, and a white picket fence around it. At the gate, holding two pistols, was a man.

Albert pushed me away with his elbow, out of the line of them pistols, and the Springfield fell off his shoulder and into his hands, neat as you please, and he fired.

The shot hit the man in the head, and the head went to pieces, like a sack full of straw. It caught on the wind and was whirled away.

The headless man did not fall.

We eased over there, and seen what we should have known. It was Wild Bill Hickok. Billy Bob had tricked us. We had announced ourselves and come into pistol range.

The shutters at the top of the church flung open, and there was Blue Hat. I seen him good in the lightning flash, just before everything went dark, and in that instant he fired, and I jerked my pistol up and fired at where I thought he was.

Blue Hat's shot was a good one. It hit Albert in the shoulder and he dropped the Springfield and went to his knees with a groan.

When lightning flashed again, I seen that I had missed Blue Hat. I probably hadn't even hit the church.

I tried to fire again, but before I could, Albert had pulled that Mex's pistol and took a shot.

Blue Hat's head popped back, his hat tossed off, then he rocked forward out the window, his pants legs catching on the sill, keeping him hanging until they ripped and he dropped on his head with a sound like a washer-woman slapping out wet laundry on a rock.

The wide, double doors were kicked open then, and there was Billy Bob, looking just like one of them jaspers in a dime novel. He had a pistol in either hand and he was blazing.

Albert had just got back on his feet, and now he was hit a bunch of times. He went backwards, dancing on one foot before he fell in the mud. As he fell, the pistol flew out of his hand and hit me in the side of the head.

I did a little crawfish shuffle, and it was like that lick woke me up, made me crazy.

When lightning flashed again and I seen Billy Bob, I yelled, "Wild Bill," and jerked a shot at him.

Then things went dark again. I stood there with my pistol pointing it where he had been, waiting, and when there was another flash, I seen him. He was lying on the ground. Somehow, I'd hit him.

He got up on his knees and started screaming at me, something about the head of his father and death to all niggers.

Then, before it could go dark again, there came a cut of lightning so thick and long, it was darn near bright as high noon.

I shot at him again.

And missed.

But he didn't.

He fired twice, and had he not been hurt, I don't figure they'd have been wounds but kill hits. One shot tore my right shoulder and the other hit me low and in the left side. I sort of melted to the ground.

That long chain of lightning finally played out, and while it was dark, I wallowed around in the mud, trying to get turned back toward the church, and trying to find my pistol or the one Albert had tossed.

Then there was lightning again.

Billy Bob wobbled to his feet, staggered for the gate. He was coming to finish me at close range. It seemed just as well to me right then. I hurt something awful.

The storm turned wilder and the lightning did like before, only really noisy this time, sizzling like bacon in a hot pan, and it was so bright it hurt my eyes.

And then there was someone beside Billy Bob. I didn't see where he came from, probably out of the woods and leaped the gate, but I thought at first it was a man in a buffalo coat. But it was Rot Toe.

Rot Toe hooted and slapped his chest with both hands, stretching tall as he could. Billy Bob stepped back, shot the ape in the chest.

Rot Toe didn't even slow down. He ran at Billy Bob and grabbed him in a hug, pinning Billy Bob's arms and pistols to his sides.

Finally the light went away, and it was dark for some time before it flashed again, and now it came in short bursts, one right after the other.

Rot Toe had Billy Bob by the back of the collar now, and was dragging him. He reached the vine-covered latticework beside the door and started up it, dragging Billy Bob with him.

Wild Bill Daniels still had his pistols, and he was trying to turn and get a shot at Rot Toe, but the way the ape was holding him, he couldn't get twisted for it.

When the ape had him halfway up the church, Billy Bob finally managed to get turned enough to shoot Rot Toe in the foot.

Rot Toe went wild, scuttled up on the latticework, some of it cracking beneath him, then he jumped for the open loft doors, hit with one foot on the sill, and caught the roof with his other hand. He never let go of Billy Bob with the other, and Billy Bob never let go of them damn pistols.

Rot Toe swung hard and up onto the roof, cranking Billy Bob up after him. When Billy Bob's boots touched the roof, he tried to get them under him, but he couldn't. Rot Toe, using one arm and his feet, started climbing the steeple.

They reached the top, and hanging by one hand to the cross. Rot Toe began to flap Billy Bob against the steeple with all his might, screeching all the while. The wind was so high, I reckoned it would blow them off, but Rot Toe held.

The sky got full of lightning again, that long-lasting, sizzling kind, and the wind howled louder than Rot Toe could screech.

Billy Bob's head slipped down inside his shirt, and it looked like he was going to drop out of it. I could just see the top of his head and his eyes.

Trying for a shot, Billy Bob arched his back against the steeple, pressed the soles of his boots against it, and pointed his pistols over his shoulders.

They clicked empty.

Billy Bob cussed.

And a long, ugly streak of lightning reached out of the sky and hit those pistols, turned them silver, lit up Rot Toe and Billy Bob bright as a harvest moon.

Then it was over. The smoking meat that had been Rot Toe and Billy Bob fell to the churchyard.

That was all for Wild Bill Daniels and Rot Toe the wrestling chimpanzee, and when I closed my feverish eyelids and heard the sound of thunder in my head, smelled the sulphur of lightning, I reckoned that it was all for me too.

Chapter Eight

I reckoned wrong.

I wasn't dead, just wished I was.

"You still alive?" It was Sled Driver.

"I think so," I said. "What about Albert?"

"I don't know," Sled Driver said. "He didn't get hit in the head this time."

He dropped me back in the mud. A moment later he was back.

"Sucker's still alive," he said. "Toughest damn nigger I ever seen. And you ain't so bad yourself, boy."

Things got sort of hazy after that, but what pretty much happened was Sled Driver got us out of the rain and someone did some doctoring on us, and neither of us went belly up.

And the crowd didn't hold no grudge. Them vultures had them a new hero to suck after.

Me.

Didn't make no never mind that I hadn't killed Billy Bob or Blue Hat, it was enough I'd outdrawn them — or that's the way Sled Driver told it. He'd been lying on his belly across the way and said he'd seen it all. I reckon he had his face down in the mud most of the time hiding from hot lead, but what the hell, he wanted to tell it that way, that was okay with me. Mud Creek liked its heroes, and right then I was just glad to be in out of the rain and patched up.

Riley was even friendly. He came over next day and had me carried outside in a wicker chair and put up against the wall. They took my picture with the Mex's pistol, which I'd never used, then they took pictures of what was left of Billy Bob and Rot Toe, and the best looking of the group cause he wasn't burned up, Blue Hat. They even dragged old Jack over for a picture, then they took him out of there quick, as he wasn't smelling any better than before. Worse maybe. You see, that storm had gone on its way about the time Billy Bob died, and it had turned off sunny and hot. And the next day, the day they took the pictures, it was even sunnier and hotter. It was darn near turning the mud to powder, and it was heating up Jack something awful. Well, you know what I mean.

Some might say that it turning off clear that quick wasn't nothing more than East Texas weather, but I'd say that curse played its self out after it got what it came for. Billy Bob.

Wasn't a whole lot of praise given Albert, as you might figure. They didn't even let him stay where I was staying, as it was for white folks. But they treated him good, and Albert said later that where he was didn't have near as many rats as you'd expect.

Riley even went over and seen how he was doing and told him to get well soon. He didn't go as far as to ask him to have a drink with him or invite him to hang around the saloon when he was well, though. Riley had to cling to some standards, even if I was the hero of the hour and Albert, as Riley said, "belonged" to me.

Isn't much more to tell. I just lived out the lie for about a week until I was over the pneumonia — which was why I'd had such a fever—and my wounds had healed a mite. When I could get around on a cane, I talked some of the townsfolk into going out to the garbage dump and bringing back the bodies of Rot Toe and Skinny. When Skinny started stinking the Magic Wagon up, and finally the town, they had all they wanted of him and hauled him off to join the garbage.

Billy Bob and Hickok—minus his head—they bothered to bury in the clearing where we'd had our show that day.

I don't know what they done with Homer, Blue Hat, and Texas Jack, but I sort of figure on the garbage dump.

I paid a grave digger some bottles of Cure-All to put Skinny and Rot Toe down next to Billy Bob, and I gave him some more to dig Billy Bob up so I could put all his dime novels in there with him. I also put in a couple of Billy Bob's spare pistols, and I made sure the books about Hickok were set on what was left of his chest. When Albert was healed up enough to travel, we got out of there, lest another gunfighter come to town or Riley set me up against some fool with a pistol.

Me and Albert never did go back to Mud Creek, but once we were back in East Texas doing our show—doing it without a wrestling chimpanzee and a shooting act—we heard that one night the town caught fire and burned slap to the ground. That seemed fair.

Oh, I forgot to tell you. On the day Albert and me left Mud Creek, we stopped off at the graves as we went out. I made a cross out of those sideboards that had the Indian spirits in them, and I put it at the head of the mounds, dead center. On it I scratched deep with my pocketknife all their names, though I didn't know Skinny's real one, and wrote:

HERE LIES A BUNCH OF FOLKS AND ONE
CRITTER THAT LIVED OUT A DIME NOVEL.

I don't know about you, but that seems about right to me.